CHANGE ME

"The girl feels the kisses he gives and goes pink. Then, lifting shy eyes toward the light, she sees at once both lover and sky" —*Pygmalion*

Etruscan sarcophagus lid, volcanic stone, late 4th early 3rd century BCE

CHANGE ME

Stories of Sexual Transformation from Ovid

JANE ALISON

Foreword by Elaine Fantham
Introduction by Alison Keith

New York   Oxford
OXFORD UNIVERSITY PRESS

Oxford University Press is a department of the University of Oxford.
It furthers the University's objective of excellence in research,
scholarship, and education by publishing worldwide.

Oxford   New York
Auckland   Cape Town   Dar es Salaam   Hong Kong   Karachi
Kuala Lumpur   Madrid   Melbourne   Mexico City   Nairobi
New Delhi   Shanghai   Taipei   Toronto

With offices in
Argentina   Austria   Brazil   Chile   Czech Republic   France   Greece
Guatemala   Hungary   Italy   Japan   Poland   Portugal   Singapore
South Korea   Switzerland   Thailand   Turkey   Ukraine   Vietnam

For titles covered by Section 112 of the US Higher Education
Opportunity Act, please visit www.oup.com/us/he for the latest
information about pricing and alternative formats.

Published by Oxford University Press
198 Madison Avenue, New York, New York 10016
http://www.oup.com

Library of Congress Cataloging-in-Publication Data
Ovid, 43 B.C.–17 A.D. or 18 A.D., author.
   Change me : stories of sexual transformation from Ovid / translated
by Jane Alison ; with a foreword by Elaine Fantham and an introduction
by Alison Keith.
      pages cm
   Includes bibliographical references.
   ISBN 978-0-19-994165-0
   1. Erotic poetry, Latin—Translations into English. 2. Latin poetry—Translations
into English. I. Alison, Jane, 1961- II. Ovid, 43 B.C.–17 A.D. or 18 A.D.
Metamorphoses. Selections. English. 2014. III. Ovid, 43 B.C.–17 A.D. or
18 A.D. Amores. Selections. English. 2014. IV. Title.
   PA6522.A2   2014
   871'.01—dc23

                                                        2013028110

Printing number: 9 8 7 6 5 4 3 2 1

Printed in the United States of America
on acid-free paper

Contents

About the Translator

JANE ALISON's previous works on Ovid include her first novel, *The Love-Artist* (2001), and a song-cycle entitled *XENIA* (with composer Thomas Sleeper, 2010). Other books are a memoir, *The Sisters Antipodes* (2009), and two novels, *The Marriage of the Sea* (2003) and *Natives and Exotics* (2005). She has an A.B. in Classics from Princeton University and an M.F.A. in Creative Writing from Columbia University and is Professor of English at the University of Virginia.

About the Contributors

ELAINE FANTHAM was educated at Oxford and taught at the University of Toronto for many years before her appointment as Giger Professor of Latin at Princeton University (1986–2000). She has published commentaries, articles, and translations of Latin poetry including Ovid *Fasti IV* (1998); an introductory study of *Metamorphoses* (2004); and most recently, a second, expanded edition *of Roman Literary Culture from Plautus to Macrobius*.

ALISON KEITH teaches Classics and Women and Gender Studies at the University of Toronto. She has written extensively on the intersection of gender and genre in Latin literature and on Ovid's *Metamorphoses* and its reception. A past Editor of the classics journal *Phoenix* (2002–2007) and President of the Classical Association of Canada (2010–2012), she has held fellowships at Clare Hall in Cambridge, Freiburg Universität in Germany, and the National Humanities Center in North Carolina.

On the Compilation and Translation

When I first read Ovid, I was nineteen and amazed that this Roman man, two thousand years earlier, could portray so precisely the dynamics of my own obsession with a beautiful but ice-cold boy. In *Metamorphoses*, one story Ovid tells is that of Echo and Narcissus: Echo is a nymph who can't speak on her own but only repeats the last words she hears; she seems helplessly needy—without a real *self*—and falls for her perfect counterpart, Narcissus, who is beautiful and adored by many, but self-contained to a deadly fault. Echo follows him and misunderstands his words, believing that he wants her as much as she does him, but he wants no one and rejects her coldly. She withers away in mortification until nothing is left but petrified bones and a floating voice. Narcissus, meanwhile, falls into a fascination with his own detached image, his reflection, and slowly wastes away as well. Like Echo, I followed the boy I knew helplessly, so unnerved in his presence I could barely speak. But he, like Narcissus, needed no one. The pain I felt that year was excruciating, yet Ovid's story seemed a gemlike portrait of my situation, giving it form, beauty, and perspective. In his *Amores*, too—the first poems he published—was line after line I felt I already knew: "I'm unable to live either with or without you / and don't seem to know what I want."[1] The stories in *Metamorphoses*, the poems in *Amores*: these miniature emblems of life made by an artist from a vastly different time still seemed, in myriad ways, true.[2]

If the poems in *Amores* document in (quasi-) realist manner the shifting passions and emotions of a narrator who shares Ovid's name and is in love with a girl he calls Corinna, the kaleidoscopic stories in *Metamorphoses* tell of transformations that seem fantastic—girls turn into birds or trees, men become mountains—but often speak of change that is likewise real. When we're young we watch as hair sprouts between our legs or as breasts swell on our chests; older, we see our skin wither: our human mutability is one of the real subjects of Ovid's fabulist book. Changes that can be most powerful are those that articulate us as sexual beings, and these Ovid—who in his *Amores* had already written so well of love, sexual games, and torment—paints best: the anxiety about having your body pierced by another; the awful desire to melt into someone; the misery of living in the wrong sexual form. He might have included Callisto's story in his *Metamorphoses* because of her magical transformations (she becomes a bear and then a constellation), but before these, she undergoes a sequence of human changes: from virgin to pregnant woman to mother. She and Ovid's Daphne, Narcissus, and Pygmalion have haunted Western thought for two millennia because they contain so many truths about natural human conditions and changes, and they speak especially seductively now because Ovid's vision is rich with moral ambiguity, psychological intensity, and wit. He is almost postmodern.

Many of the stories of sexual encounter in the *Metamorphoses* are charged by unnerving questions not of what is right but of what one could do. Myrrha, for instance, is sexually obsessed with her father. She tries to fight this but finally gives in, reasoning that, among other cultures and animals, sires often mate with their offspring, so what's wrong if she sleeps with her father? Only arbitrary convention, she tells herself. There is nothing wrong, her desire is natural, and to deny it would in fact be perverse. So she creeps into her father's bedroom when her mother is away ... Ovid studied law before giving in to his brilliance as a poet. His skills of persuasion express a questioning of norms and authority that can seem utterly contemporary. At the same time, his narratives can be imbued with astonishing psychological astuteness: in a complex poem like *Am.* 3.11, in which the speaker struggles with violently shifting emotions, and in a story like "Myrrha," he comes close to modern psychological portraiture.

Ovid's stories melt moral conventions, explore ambiguities, dissolve boundaries between men, women, animals, gods, plants, and the mineral world, and in doing so they can be moving—but even more often witty or shocking: they contrive to seduce the reader, often despite herself. It is curious and unnerving to be drawn into a story of a girl like Europa, who is smitten by a white bull on a beach. And horrifying to see a girl raped and her tongue cut out—but then gruesomely comic to see that severed tongue creep to the feet of its mistress. And it's fascinating to see a switch on the usual dynamic when a young woman attacks a boy: Salmacis craves Hermaphroditus, who's made the mistake of swimming naked in her pool. She plunges in after him, seizes him, and will not let him go, violently fusing her body with his until the two become a new two-sexed being. Ovid's dark pleasure in telling such stories with a full register of tones is palpable, and he leaves a reader with images—a woman entangling a boy like an octopus, a girl caressing the horn of a bull as it carries her away—printed in the brain.

Although Ovid drew upon countless sources and worked with different genres for his rendition of myths in *Metamorphoses*, they are far from "retellings":[3] they're infused with his sensibility as a self-conscious artist, with his delight in seducing and disturbing, but also with deeply serious questioning. What does it mean to have thoughts and passions trapped inside a changeable body? What is a *self*, and where are its edges? If someone can pierce you in sex and in love, how do you survive? And if your outer form changes, what lasts?

We don't know exactly why Ovid was exiled from Rome (a poem and an error, he says), but his literary fascination with transgression, his testing of boundaries, and his constant questioning that destabilizes all that seems fixed, surely had something to do with it—but also helped make his work last.

ON THE SELECTIONS

The seven selections here from *Amores* offer a miniature of the dramas, shifting tones, and narrative shape of that collection, from the narrator's first finding a form—both the form of love poetry and the form of a girl, Corinna—to his anxiety upon "publishing" both. Along the way he moves through adoration, jealousy, rage, and exhaustion, the tone likewise shifting from wickedly provocative to seemingly earnest. In addition to giving a sense of the whole *Amores*, these selections can offer synaptical connections with the subsequent stories from *Metamorphoses*. The opening assertion in the first poem here from *Amores*—that the narrator has been ensnared by a girl—must be seen in the light of the many cases in *Metamorphoses* in which a young girl is literally the prey of a man or god and is drastically altered when caught, or changes to escape being caught, losing her form, her self, her self-expression. Indeed, a theme running through the veins of *Metamorphoses* is how the self is expressed by language and, more pointedly, can no longer be expressed by language after transformation into a bear, stream, or tree. *Amores* also explores ideas of linguistic or coded communication, but in the more realistic and ironic zone of lovers in Rome. They write silent words in wine and exchange nods and secret messages, or they helplessly witness these traded by others—all of which resonates with the many nonvoiced expressions in the fantastical stories of *Metamorphoses*: Philomela's weaving, the words silently murmured by Narcissus' reflection, Io's hoof-printed name, Daphne's ambiguous nod as a tree. Further, the catalogues of fantastical things that poets can do, in *Amores* 1.3 and 3.12, offer a plank from the realistic zone of those poems to the fabulist stories that follow.

Crucial to *Metamorphoses* is the complex shape of the entire poem—Ovid called it a *carmen perpetuum*, an unending song or constant enchantment—in which stories are nested within other stories or glide one to another almost imperceptibly. Ovid wove a shimmering and shape-shifting whole. But this present volume, as a selection, has dissolved the poem's overall texture and ingenious construction. Most of the stories here reveal edges that bleed a little where they've been ripped from another just before or after, so that you will often enter a narrative not yet knowing who is speaking or to whom the names refer. In these translations, those bleeding edges have not been cauterized: it's important to remain aware of the body from which the stories came. Endnotes following the translations, however, will give this context (notes are keyed by line number).

In several cases you can sew the original fabric together again with carefully sequenced reading: in *Metamorphoses*, the story of Actaeon, for instance, leads into that of Semele, which leads to that of Tiresias, and from there, to Echo and Narcissus. The stories of Pygmalion, Myrrha, and Adonis (sung by Orpheus) are likewise joined. Although they appear out of Ovid's order here, you can read them in the original sequence instead for a sense of the pattern.

On the categories in which these stories have been grouped: to fix any of Ovid's stories in a single slot is like trying to carry water in a sieve. I took a cue from his own artist, Arachne, who, in the cloth she weaves in her contest with Minerva, creates a cluster of stories to make a point (*argumentum*, 6.69), involving incidents of male gods deceiving or raping women. In this collection, likewise, the categories focus on defining incidents or topics, such as rape or incest. But, of course, many of these stories resist clear distinctions. Semele's, for instance, is ostensibly about Jove's overpowering sexual potency, but Semele herself has been too potent (*potens*, 3.292) in persuading him to come to her as he does to Juno. He tries to restrain his potency but doesn't seem to have that power, and Semele, already pregnant, is immolated by him. But where she thus fails to be a mother, Jove performs, by snatching the unborn child from her ruined body and sewing it into his leg until its "mother-time"—*materna tempora* (3.312)—is over and the baby is ready to be born. Thus the "victim" in the story is victim first of her own potency, and the most potently male god becomes quasi-female. Does this story belong in the category of "ruining" or of "switching"? Even more slippery: when Salmacis watches a boy swim naked in her pool, then plunges in after him, and the two fuse as a single new figure, is this "looking," "taking," "ruining," or "switching"? All of them. Because in this case of forced sex, it's a female bending a male to her will, I thought it most illuminating to set it among the other "taking" stories. But an argument could be made for any of the other categories, and maybe such a conversation will be had by those who read this.

The *Metamorphoses* selections begin with the story of Arachne, noted earlier. She does "look" at sex and is ostensibly punished for this (and her talent) by being turned into a spider, but her tale also works as one of several mirrors of Ovid's larger text and thus can remind a reader of the original texture of the whole (as well as itself being pre-mirrored in the "catalogues" of myth in *Amores*).[4] Not only does the young weaver, like Ovid, choose a set of incidents that are thematically related, but her artistry mimics his as well:

> illic et Tyrium quae purpura sensit aenum
> texitur et tenues parvi discriminis umbrae;
> qualis ab imbre solent percussis solibus arcus

inficere ingenti longum curvamine caelum;
in quo diversi niteant cum mille colores,
transitus ipse tamen spectantia lumina fallit:
usque adeo, quod tangit, idem est; tamen ultima distant.

Woven in is purple concocted in Tyrian pots
and delicate shades that invisibly shift,
as when sunrays shine through a shower of rain
and a rainbow curves color across the wide sky;
in it glows the whole spectrum of hues,
but from one to the next a haze fools our eyes.
Each shade like the next, but the ends: so distant!   (6.61–67)

The near-invisible shading from one story to the next makes any one plucked from the whole seem to fray, yet setting stories newly alongside each other also lets light shine on connections among them. When Philomela weaves her story to tell her sister that she was raped and muted, a reader will surely think of Arachne. Watching Pygmalion soften his ivory girl to life might take one back to Narcissus, whose desire within him melts its object (his own icy self), leaving a flower that is a pictorial record—a yellow heart ringed by white—as well as to Salmacis, gazing hotly at the ivory boy in her pool. To see Io print her name in the sand might remind a reader of Apollo's words of grief written on the new hyacinth flower, Byblis' letter to her brother and the pains she took to write it, Iphis' gender-switching inscription of thanks, and back again to Philomela . . .

With thematic regrouping we can also see Ovid's tactics to differentiate within a genus of stories. Both Myrrha and Byblis, for instance, have incestuous longings—for father or brother—and both engage in extended interior monologues that show Ovid's psychological acumen and his rhetorical training.[5] To wrestle the matter further, Myrrha acquires a physical external agent in the person of her old nurse, while Byblis *creates* an abstracted external agent in the form of the letter she writes to her brother. Both characters threaten suicide if they don't get what they want, but Myrrha—again, physical—actually tries to hang herself, whereas Byblis keeps her threat verbal, urging her brother not to be cited in her epitaph as the cause of death. And within the arguments each young woman wages with herself, the two differ crucially: Myrrha cites examples of incestuous mating within the animal world, while Byblis cites cases within the divine world. Both are questioning the seeming arbitrariness of human custom between the poles of animal and divine—and by extension, questioning what it means to be human, having conscious spirit within animal flesh. Reading the two side by side makes Ovid's ingenious treatment of the two stories all the more pronounced.[6]

As a narrative artist, Ovid was, above all, concerned with the large design of the work but also with the energies operating within each story. He wrote when fictional narrative was more likely to be found in verse than in prose: he was as much storyteller as poet. Although he drew widely from earlier accounts of myth in constructing the stories of *Metamorphoses*, he also invented enormously: in some instances, such as "Echo and Narcissus," binding different stories that had probably not been linked before.[7] But whether newly fleshing the old skeleton of a story or frankensteining something new from parts, in each case Ovid had to make the narrative *live*. At a certain point he was a writer, alone, struggling with one word after another, like Arachne choosing one colored thread after another. As a fiction writer translating his stories, experiencing them at a pace far closer to writing than to reading, I've been drawn to fundamental aspects of his narrative composition: how he propelled each piece, held it together, and gave it a sense of ending (or refused to).

Something that becomes clear at once is how economically staged they can be. Quickly Ovid paints in the main figures, their situation and place, perhaps the barest notes about their past, and above all what one of them wants. Then motion begins and develops through an interplay between things done and things thought—desires, fears, the net of inner conflicts, revealed through dialogue or soliloquy—all advancing the narrative quickly. What impels most of Ovid's stories here (indeed most stories, in one way or another[8]) is desire. Desire to have something, or escape something, or punish, or know: desire within the characters, and desire within the reader. Want is like the flue of a chimney, pulling upward a current of air and keeping the flames alive. Ovid starts most of his stories with a condition of crackling potential, and then he lights the match. Apollo, for instance, sees and is kindled with desire (thanks to Cupid) for a girl he then pursues. But desire needs resistance in narrative: Apollo might badly want a girl, but one way for there to be a story is if she just as badly does *not* want him. This is the friction that keeps the story moving, this simple system of desire and counter-desire until the situation is resolved or exhausted, the conditions have changed to a new form of (temporary) stasis: the girl escapes rape by becoming a tree; the god settles on having only her leaves as his emblem—although the ambiguity at the end of this tale keeps some subtle tension within the reader.

Although the *Metamorphoses* is full of rapes, it's not only females who are "taken," and, indeed, female figures in Ovid are often agents of their own change. Salmacis hunts and transforms the boy she wants; Myrrha pursues her father; Byblis propositions her brother; Europa, following her desire for that beautiful bull, is more an agent of her change than the Daphnes and Callistos of the narrative, yet even they are huntresses, in the business of tracking and taking, and it is Daphne herself, when chased by Apollo, who begs her father: "Change me."

Another story in which a girl is pursued yet still functions actively is "Arethusa." One of the poem's many hunter girls, she rouses the lust of a river-god when she swims in his waters, and finds herself hunted by him. She runs, naked and terrified, until finally, when he traps her, with Diana's help she melts into a stream to escape him. An important element of this story is that Arethusa launches the motion with her desire: she's hot from her own hunting and wants water. And she isn't happy just to dip her feet in water; she wants to plunge in and be altered. This desire, on which she acts, triggers the river-god's counter-desire, which in turn triggers *her* counter-desire to flee until the story reaches the ultimate fulfillment of what technically had started it: Arethusa's desire to be enveloped in cool water. She at last turns into a stream. So, her longing for water is indeed met. Further, she is telling her own story (even if, in this case, she's telling her story within a nest of stories told by other narrators).

The more figures in a story, the more complex the system of desire, as in the long tale of Philomela: here one figure's desire leads to another's in what becomes a full ecology. Procne, recently married, longs to see her sister, Philomela; Procne's husband, Tereus, longs to please his wife so goes to fetch Philomela. Upon seeing her, though, he suddenly craves her for himself; not knowing this, she in turn wants to go with him to see her sister, so here two unlike desires are hideously confluent. Once he has Philomela in his domain, Tereus rapes her, cuts out her tongue, and locks her up. This violence in turn launches Philomela's desire to tell the crime to her sister and find a way to do so. Once Procne learns what's happened, she has a fresh desire, that is, to punish her husband, and so on. The story is structured by a sequence of wants like flame passed from torch to torch. Each want is born of a human relation somewhere on the scale from "natural" to "unnatural," and it moves from what seems most conventional—a sister's desire to see her loved sister—to what seems most disruptive—a man raping and muting his sister-in-law, a mother murdering her child. At this point of mutual castration and extinction, the story's system of desires has exhausted itself and ends in ruin.

Ovid finds more subtle ways to signal an end, too. In "Echo and Narcissus," for instance, in addition to the natural conclusion of the two principals' twin lines of desire, he works in other elements to give this sense. The question of whether and how Tiresias' prophetic words might be true starts the story, and by the end this question has been answered. The story's deeper origins are in water, where Narcissus' mother Liriope is raped and conceives him, and not only does Narcissus' central drama focus upon water, but we again enter water at the end (now with irony), when he gazes at himself in the Styx. Echo makes an early appearance in the story to reflect the desirability of Narcissus, and she reappears near the end to usher him out of life. A similar balance exists in the wider chorus who longed for him in the opening passages and reappear to grieve him at the end. All these subtle balancing elements work like a sweet at the end of a meal, signaling to our bodies that it's over.

ON THE TRANSLATION

Translator Burton Raffel puts the problem bluntly: no two languages having the same phonology, syntactical structure, vocabulary, literary history, or prosody, it's impossible to re-create these aspects of a literary work composed in one language into another.[9] In *NOX*, a chimaera of literary and visual forms, Anne Carson speaks of translation as "a room . . . where one gropes for the light switch":

> Prowling the meanings of a word, prowling the history
> of a person, no use expecting a flood of light. Human
> words have no main switch. But all those little
> kidnaps in the dark. And then the luminous, big,
> shivering, discandied, unrepentant, barking web of
> them that hangs in your mind when you turn back to
> the page you were trying to translate.[10]

When working on these selections (for which I've used R. J. Tarrant's 2004 Oxford edition of *Metamorphoses* and E. J. Kenney's 1995 Oxford edition of *Amores*; brackets before line numbers mean that I've followed those editors' suggested deletions of lines from the manuscript), I was especially interested in trying to capture Ovid's shifting narrative speeds. As his characters move through their fantastical world, and his printed characters move across the page, things change, and they change at speeds Ovid controls. The time it takes to absorb these changes—that is, the pacing of both his metrical feet and his figures' feet (see Iphis)—was something I wanted to catch. He uses the full spectrum of speeds as modern authors know them, with gaps that leap over implied incident; supercondensed summary; quickened narration in sentences full of parataxis; scenes that move in "real time"; lengthy descriptions that dilate a moment for aesthetic effect or tension;[11] and intrusions of exposition or commentary (*sententiae*) that freeze movement altogether.

On his flying narration, even of a moment that's not action packed, here's an example of parataxis from the story of Byblis, once she's begun writing the fatal letter to her brother:

> incipit et dubitat; scribit damnatque tabellas;
> et notat et delet; mutat culpatque probatque,

inque vicem sumptas ponit positasque resumit.

She starts but doubts, writes, can't stand what she's written,
makes a mark, rubs it out, revises, loathes, tries again,
puts down what she's taken up, takes up what she's put down.   (9.523–5)

And here is a passage at the start of "Adonis," where Ovid begins with a brief piece of static commentary, then in four lines races over perhaps twenty years, slows again for four lines of closer narration that cover a moment and its conse-quence, then skips over crucial information—when did Venus first see Adonis; how did the affair begin?—for another rapid passage summarizing several months:

Labitur occulte fallitque uolatilis aetas,
et nihil est annis uelocius. ille sorore   520
natus auoque suo, qui conditus arbore nuper,
nuper erat genitus, modo formosissimus infans,
iam iuuenis, iam uir, iam se formosior ipso est;
iam placet et Veneri matrisque ulciscitur ignes.
namque pharetratus dum dat puer oscula matri,   525
inscius exstanti destrinxit harundine pectus.
laesa manu natum dea reppulit; altius actum
uulnus erat specie primoque fefellerat ipsam.
capta uiri forma non iam Cythereia curat
litora, non alto repetit Paphon aequore cinctam   530
piscosamque Cnidon grauidamque Amathunta metallis.
abstinet et caelo; caelo praefertur Adonis.

Time glides by in secret, so swift we can't see:
nothing's quicker than years. That child of his own   520
grandfather and sister, first hidden in a tree,
then born, and then the most lovely baby,
is now boy, now man, now more lovely than himself.
He pleases Venus, too, pays back his mother's flames.
For as the boy with arrows gives his mother a kiss,   525
by mistake an arrow peeks out, grazing her breast.
The goddess is stung and thrusts him away; the cut
is deeper than it seems, and she herself is fooled.
Undone by a man's beauty, she stops attending
Cythera's beaches, won't go to Paphos edged by sea,   530

(10.519–32) fish-filled Cnidos, or Amathus laden with copper.
She stays far from heaven—heaven, if there's Adonis?

Other tricks Ovid uses for speed from line to line: his preference for lighter dactyls (words of three syllables, the first long and the next two short) rather than slower spondees (words of two long syllables); his avoidance of elision (between words, not incidents!), which can weigh down syllables; and his use of enjambment, starting a new clause or phrase near the end of a line and running it over the break. He also abbreviates the entries into and exits from reported speech, and his quick shifts in tone add to the darting sense of the narrative.[12]

But Ovid carefully controls slowness, too, as in the many ruminative passages, when Narcissus, Myrrha, Iphis, and Scylla struggle with themselves. Here the motion is in the exposition or argument, deep and meandering, the effect more like a piece of moiré cloth being slowly turned about in the light. What changes in such passages is the character's mind.

Translation is a slow process, during which one dwells on a single word for weeks and becomes acutely aware when the same word or family of words recurs in a brief text, a choice that must reflect how Ovid, as he set about his complex weaving, might have invented or found words that were kernels around which significant aspects of the story organically formed. In "Myrrha," for instance, a central word is *nomen*, or name. It is the last word of the story leading to Myrrha's (10.297) and the first word of the last line of her story (10.502); it also appears on lines 10.346, 358, 366, 439, 467, 468—together with the related concept, that of speaking or not speaking a nonproper name for a relation, in this case "father" or "daughter" (lines 10.366, 422, 429). As this story reveals, a person's proper name (giving her identity and individuality) and the relational name (establishing family ties within a system of human order) are ephemeral, a matter of breath and sound that, if not spoken, can obliterate both identity and order. The last line and a half of the story are usually translated something like, "Men call [the drops] myrrh; no age will ever forget the word" (Humphries), or "from the trunk the weeping myrrh / Keeps on men's lips for aye the name of her" (Melville). But, given that the disaster in this story comes from Myrrha's name not being spoken when it should have been—when her nurse arranges the rendezvous with her father, calling Myrrha by a false name (*nomine mentito*, 10.439)—I've chosen to stress differently the crucial word *tacebitur* in the last line and translate the passage this way: "the myrrh wept by the bark / keeps the girl's name, which will never be left unsaid."

Other points of translation: to give some sense of Ovid's speed and the time it takes to move through his narrative, I wanted to create lines of roughly the same length as his and rhythms that might come close. Time passes as a reader absorbs each word and line, and this sense of time I've tried to retain. His "golden" lines—two adjectives, a verb, two nouns—are all but impossible to re-create, but now and then a compacted line tries. Ditto regarding his alliteration, near-rhyme, and mirrored word positioning (as in "Echo and Narcissus," especially). Latin vocabulary is more limited than English, but it has more flexible syntax; I've taken license in using different English words where Latin is limited (*flamma, niveus*), to balance the languages.

Although Ovid often starts his stories in a past-perfect tense for backstory, he subsequently switches—presumably for metrical reasons—between simple past and present tenses. Each sounds natural to the modern ear, although the newly chronic use of the present tense in contemporary fiction has brought attention to its weaknesses,[13] and shifts between tenses can jar. I haven't always followed Ovid's shifts but have slid between tenses, too, when the mood, speed, or pictorial quality of the passage seems to ask for one tense or the other. Something that can bewilder a modern reader is Ovid's exotic ways of naming that don't identify figures or places easily. This he does for meter, erudition, variety, and fun. To replicate or translate? I've done a little of both. He also has elaborate ways of denoting time, which usually involve the position of the sun or moon or constellations: because these have altered the way I look at the moon, I've translated most of these time-renderings literally. Finally, some translators have ignored Ovid's frequent use of apostrophe—that is, when he suddenly switches to second person and addresses a character—as something that contemporary readers aren't used to. But this does not seem true in our postmodern world, so I've retained many of those curious addresses.

The stories of sexuality translated here and the constellation of poems from *Amores* that precede them are as compelling now as they were two thousand years ago, and what they reveal of gender, and of minds and hearts inside bodies in the ancient world is extraordinarily rich.[14] I hope this new selection will bring Ovid and his vision to many more readers, especially younger people who might glimpse themselves in the shifting characters that pace these pages. I hope, too, that this new selection might seduce new readers to climb on the bull's back and plunge into Ovid's full works.

---

*The reader's experience with Change Me is further enriched by a companion website, www.oup.com/us/alison, which includes audio files of key passages that I read aloud (indicated in the text by an icon placed in the margin).

Notes

1. For a brilliant discussion of this self-division in love that goes back at least as far as Sappho, see Anne Carson's *Eros the Bittersweet* (Princeton: Princeton University Press, 1986).

2. As Segal notes, "The pervading trope of the *Metamorphoses* rests on the premise that its world of myth and art can convert into physical form some underlying quality of mind, character, or emotion, whether these are a lasting feature of personality or a transient mood or emotion. It is a corollary of this premise that through this mechanism of physical convertibility the poet can reveal the hidden essence of a personality—its needs, longings, passions, fears—in a form that is closely tied to the physicality of the body" (12). Charles Segal, "Ovid's Metamorphic Bodies: Art, Gender, and Violence in the *Metamorphoses*," *Arion*, 3rd series, 5, no. 3 (Winter 1998): 9–41.

3. Keith says, "As universal history, the *Metamorphoses* is also a universal literary history." Alison Keith, "Sources and Genres in Ovid's *Metamorphoses 1–5*," in *Brill's Companion to Ovid*, ed. Barbara Weiden Boyd (Leiden: Brill, 2002), 268.

4. On Arachne as one of the "miniatures" of the poem, see, for instance, Gianpiero Rosati "Narrative Techniques and Narrative Structures in the *Metamorphoses*," in *Brill's Companion*, 275–6; also Rosati's essay "Form in Motion: Weaving the Text in the *Metamorphoses*," in *Oxford Readings in Ovid*, ed. Peter Knox (New York: Oxford University Press, 2006), 335–50.

5. For a brief discussion on this, see Robert Scholes and Robert Kellogg, *The Nature of Narrative* (New York: Oxford University Press, 1966), 184–5.

6. I don't think that Ovid's treatments of the stories are, as Humphries says in the introduction to his translation of *Metamorphoses*, "almost identical" instances of relying upon cliché and fixed devices. Ovid, *Metamorphoses*, trans. Rolfe Humphries (Bloomington: Indiana University Press, 1955), viii.

7. And in the process, as Kenney puts it, creating a fusion that has "become canonical." E. J. Kenney, introduction to Ovid, *Metamorphoses*, trans. A. D. Melville (Oxford: Oxford University Press, 1986), xxiv.

8. For a discussion of this principle, see, for instance, Peter Brooks, *Reading for the Plot* (Cambridge, MA: Harvard University Press, 1984).

9. Burton Raffel, *The Art of Translating Poetry* (University Park: Pennsylvania State University Press, 1988) 12.

10. Anne Carson, *NOX* (New York: New Directions Books, 2010), 7.1.

11. See Salzman-Mitchell on descriptions, or "detentions of the story," as more "feminine" moments versus "masculine" narration: Patricia Salzman-Mitchell, "The Fixing Gaze," in *Gendered Dynamics in Latin Love Poetry*, ed. Ronnie Ancona and Ellen Greene (Baltimore: Johns Hopkins University Press, 2005), 159.

12. For discussions of some of Ovid's most notable stylistic techniques, see Kenney, introduction to Ovid, *Metamorphoses*, as well as his longer essay "Ovid's Language and Style," in *Brill's Companion*, 78–89; also W. S. Anderson's introduction to his *Ovid's Metamorphoses Books 6–10* (Norman: University of Oklahoma Press, 1972).

13. See Lynne Sharon Schwartz, "Remembrance of Tense Past," in *Writers on Writing*, ed. Robert Packer and Jay Parini (Hanover, NH: Middlebury College, 1991), 232–247; and William H. Gass, "A Failing Grade for the Present Tense," in *Finding a Form* (New York: Alfred A. Knopf, 1996), 14–30.

14. See Alison Sharrock's discussion in "Gender and Sexuality," in *Cambridge Companion*, 95–107.

Foreword

OVID: POET AND VISIONARY
Elaine Fantham

We know from Ovid's own verse autobiography (*Tristia* 4.10) that he was born in 43 BCE "when both consuls fell in battle." It must have been a dreadful year: the consuls Hirtius and Pansa had been authorized by the Senate at Cicero's instigation to join Caesar's charismatic heir Octavian in combating Mark Antony (then a public enemy) at Mutina (Modena) in northern Italy; but Hirtius and Pansa both died of wounds or sickness, and Octavian had turned around to ally himself with the public enemy and demand recognition from the Senate of their absolute powers (shared with the weak Aemilius Lepidus) as a "Board of Three to reorganize" the state for an initial five years. This Triumvirate was renewed for a second five-year period, but Octavian was no longer a Triumvir when his fleet attacked and defeated the fleet of Antony and Cleopatra at Actium in 31 BCE. The new junta had established itself in 43 by mass proscriptions, including the scholarly and apolitical Varro, whose friends helped him escape, and Cicero, who was murdered late that year.

Luckily Ovid's father was outside the privileged elite; a well-off landowner some distance from Rome among the Paeligni, and both Ovid and his elder brother were favored by Octavian (now Augustus) with the "broad band" on their togas that marked them for a public career. Ovid's brother died when he was only twenty, but Ovid held one or perhaps two junior magistracies (*Tristia* 4.10.31–36). The trouble was that he loathed public service and devoted himself to the poetry that he tells us had come spontaneously even when he first set out to write prose (ibid., 25–26).

By 27 BCE when Octavian was metamorphosed into Augustus ("The Venerable One") by the Senate's unanimous decree, Ovid was perhaps reciting some of his early poems, which he dates to the time when he shaved his first beard: certainly he soon published a five-book edition of his first work *Amores* (*Affairs of Love*), situation-based elegies ostensibly about his love life in the tradition that had established itself at Rome since Catullus composed his poems of love for "Lesbia," both long and short. Catullus' poetry of love has usually been read as real autobiography, recording his infatuation with the wealthy married Clodia

Metelli and tragic reaction to her infidelity. Whatever their basis in fact, these passionate poems started a school of Roman love poets whose works contained as much fantasy and fiction as actual memoirs: First Cornelius Gallus, the army commander, whose love poems are lost, who was honored by Virgil in his sixth and tenth Eclogues. After offending Octavian, Gallus took his own life when Ovid was a very young man. Next came Tibullus, who addressed his elegies to more than one beloved and both genders. Close after him followed Propertius, who focused his love poetry on the unique Cynthia: her name is the first word, and was used as the title, of his first volume. He would write four books, but while the third chronicles his break with Cynthia, her memory haunts the fourth book, largely concerned with the myths and causes (etiology) of Roman rituals. Cynthia returns for two powerfully dramatic recollections of their past: 4.7, where her shade appears to him in a dream, reproaching him for neglecting her burial and taking a new mistress, and 4.8, going further back to their living relationship. Cynthia has gone on a day-trip out of town with a young admirer, and Propertius is consoling himself with hired dancers and entertainers when Cynthia returns, flinging open the doors, and brings him to her feet in abject supplication.

Ovid saw himself as the last of four love poets: he tells us that he was too young to hear Tibullus but listened to Propertius recite his tales of passion (4.10. 45–46, 57–58). Certainly Propertius contributed more to the range and variety of Ovid's love poetry than any other Roman predecessor.

Our earliest examples of his quasi-autobiographical love stories survive in his *Amores*, but the poetry collection we read is not the five books he originally composed, as he tells us in his preface to the volume, but a revision in three books; although he implies that this eases the burden on his readers, the collected volume may simply have regrouped the same poems. We cannot tell whether Ovid eliminated elegies, or added them, or both added and subtracted, or simply changed their order.

To call them love poems implies to most readers poems addressed to a beloved, and Ovid refers to them as poems to or about Corinna (not, he says, her real name). But before she enters his text, he opens the collection with an account of how he started out to write serious heroic poetry, but Cupid stole the last foot from his second line, thus turning his text from epic into elegiac couplets, and shot the poet with the arrow of love. Although Ovid surrendered, he still had no subject matter, no woman to write about, until the third poem, when he addresses a new beloved: I paraphrase *Amores.* 1.3: "Accept a lover who will forever be your slave, accept a man who knows how to love in pure fidelity . . . just give me abundant material for my poems, and poems will spring forth worthy of you: Like Io, or Leda or Europa, we too will be sung together worldwide, and our names [*Nomina nostra*= mine] will forever be linked with yours."

The oddest feature of this final section is the poet's slippery use of the first person plural, moving from the fame of women loved by Jupiter not to Corinna herself, but to his own name and fame. In the following poem, Ovid can only see his beloved across the dinner table, because she is the property of another—her *Vir*, which could be either husband or recognized paramour—but in 1.5 she comes to him during the siesta hour to satisfy their desires.

We might expect this happy consummation to be unique in the collection. Surely there can only be one such poem, but Ovid will return to the glory of consummation in the next book (2.12). Successive elegies reverse or contradict each other. *Amores* 1.7 is important in showing the possibility of entering into another's pain; it is a scene of domestic violence, after which the poet curses his own hands for striking (and tearing and scratching!) his love, whom he compares to deserted heroines of mythology, picturing her pallor and trembling in terms that foreshadow several rape scenes in the *Metamorphoses*.

> Who would not have called me "Crazy," or "Barbarian?"
>> But she said nothing, fear held back her tongue.
> Yet her expression spoke her mute reproaches
>> And with her tears though silent charged me guilty   (19–22)

> She stood struck dumb with white and bloodless face
>> Like rocks of marble hewn from Parian cliffs:
> I saw her fainting arms and trembling limbs
>> Just as the breezes fan a poplar's leaves
> Or as the slender reed bends with the gentle Zephyr,
>> Or the sea-surface brushed with western wind,
> And long-welling tears flowed from her eyes
>> like water seeping from discarded snow   (51–58)

Here is real empathy with physical and emotional shock, so intense the poet can call her tears his own blood (60).

We shall often see the same empathy in the love narratives of *Metamorphoses*. But the themes and situations of many of these elegies, with their mixture of realism and wishful thinking, existed before Ovid, either compressed in the short Hellenistic epigram or developed in fuller contexts. It is not the theme that distinguishes Ovid, but his ingenious development of it.

In contrast there is comic realism in 3.7, when the poet bemoans his impotence in a recent encounter; not that the girl lacked appeal or skill in enticing him, but his penis failed him and lies inert like a log. Is this about Corinna? Not at all. He takes care to record his recent successes with three different street girls and an occasion during which he claimed nine orgasms with Corinna in one night. Is he bewitched? His impotence has disgraced him, and he scolds his member as "my worst part" for its misplaced modesty. Angered, as if he had been making fun of her, the nameless girl leaps from the bed and washes thoroughly to give the impression that they have enjoyed sex.

We can hardly read these poems so different in mood and content as if the poet were truly focused on a single relationship. Ovid enjoys paradox and inconsistency: the faithful lover can boast of his omnivorous sexual performance, and Ovid takes pains to juxtapose incompatible situations. This diversity is apparent in, for example, 2.12, the second poem exulting over of his possession of Corinna. Typically he applies metaphors of military conquest and imitates Propertius (2.25) in setting his triumph above that of Agamemnon. He contrasts the glory he has won by an unaided personal campaign with the siege of Troy and other great wars. The *casus belli* is a woman as usual, but Cupid has ordered him to campaign without slaughter. In the next poem, a condemnation of Corinna's supposed abortion, Ovid uses a series of counterfactuals, arguing that mankind would have died out and that heroes like Achilles or Romulus or Aeneas would never have been born if their mothers had practiced abortion. This is his cue for invoking the tragic myths of infanticide by Medea and Procne, which will be central narratives in *Metamorphoses*. The elegist draws color and intensity by moving from personal reaction to invoking famous tragic myths. It came naturally to Roman poets to draw analogies between their ordinary world and mythology: many young orators had been trained to compose speeches of advice to tragic or historical figures, or impersonated the speeches of actual heroes or heroines. This is the background for Ovid's other early poetic forms; his tragedy of *Medea*, his *Letters from Heroines,* and the books of mock didactic, his *Arts of Love.*

Was it the *Art of Love* that brought on Ovid's disgrace? Even in the earlier *Amores*, he protected himself from charges of adultery by affirming the fictional nature of his love life in the key elegy 3.12—as fictional as the magic tools lent by the gods of mythology to favorite heroes. After he was sent into exile in 8 CE, Ovid would blame his fate on an unidentified "error" in his past and on one of his poems (*Carmen*). In his powerful self-defense from exile (*Tristia* 2), he follows protestations of loyal good wishes for the emperor's continued success with a defense of his love poetry based on famous Greek precedents from Homer (notably Demodocus' song in *Odyssey* 8 about the adulterous love of Mars and Venus) through lyric poetry to tragedy and Roman patriotic epic. Augustus enjoyed performances of scurrilous and cheerfully immoral mime-plays and ancient comedy; Ovid cites them along with mythological statuary as proof that Rome was full of incentives to love making, both visual and literary, especially

Catullus and the elegists, whose material was as erotic as his own poetry. But he never acknowledges that there might be a difference in provocative effect between the tales of his first-person susceptibilities and full-blown affairs (*Amores*), along with the dramatized pleas of heroines, and his second-person recommendations to modern lovers for successful seduction, instructing them how to find a love object, how to win her over, and then how to keep her love. He gives the impression that it was his four didactic books on the *Art of Love,* including one addressed to women—not, he claims, to respectable wives and daughters but to women who lived by their sexuality—that had offended Augustus. Surely poems boasting of adulterous conquests and mocking husbands who defended their marital honor would offend even a ruler who had not, as Augustus had done by his marriage laws of 18 BCE, proclaimed the importance of reestablishing respect for marriage by sanctioning severe legal penalties for wifely infidelity.

It is discreet of Ovid to blame his poetry, but there were more powerful factors causing his disgrace. In 2 BCE Augustus had held this reverend title for twenty-five years; he presided over the consulship of his younger grandson Lucius Caesar, while preparing his older grandson Gaius for a showcase expedition against the Parthians to start in the following year. Now was the time for him to consent to accept the honor of "Father of His People" (*Pater patriae*), which the Senate had long been offering him.

But barely had the Father of His People celebrated his title and the opening of his new Forum and temple of Mars, when his parental claims were shamed by his only child: his daughter, Julia, was the subject of a dreadful scandal. Let us take a moment to understand Roman political marriages and the harm they inflicted on princesses. As with Latinus' only child Lavinia in Virgil's great poem, when a ruler had no son, marriage to his daughter was used to mark the husband as successor. On this principle, Augustus married Julia to each of her three husbands: the first, his nephew Marcellus, fell ill and died within the year; the second was Augustus' trusty friend Agrippa, to whom Julia bore five children. Despite subsequent gossip, this was a harmonious marriage, although largely spent away from Rome as Agrippa served as viceroy over the Asian provinces. But on Agrippa's death, Augustus imposed a third marriage on Julia, this time with his stepson Tiberius. Tiberius deeply loved his previous wife, and resentment between the new couple erupted when their baby son died. After they separated, in 6 BCE, Tiberius repudiated his public duties and left to live as a student in the free city of Rhodes. Augustus would not permit a divorce, and Julia, denied remarriage, enjoyed a scandalous life apparently known to all but her father. When Augustus heard the gossip of her five lovers and drunken parties, he was so enraged that he sent a letter to the Senate denouncing her in detail and sent her immediately and without trial into exile on the bleak island of Pandateria.

Ovid's erotic verse may have corrupted society, but it had no effect on Ovid's career until nine years later, in 8 CE, when Julia's daughter ("Julia the younger") was involved in a sex scandal in which her lover was identified and pardoned, but Julia was exiled—to another island. The baby she bore was treated as a bastard and exposed to die, and Ovid, who belonged to her smart set but is not known to have committed any illegal acts, was exiled overnight.

Why was Julia the younger's lover left unpunished, but Ovid driven to exile on the Black Sea coast? Because he knew too much? Or was it simply that the sheer increase in his popularity during this decade had correspondingly increased Augustus' resentment?

There is still another possibility: during these same years, Ovid began to write his *Metamorphoses,* which he tells us was all but finished when he was sent away. Could the *carmen* that was his major offense be *Metamorphoses* rather than the erotic poetry? A prominent framing feature of the great epic poem is Ovid's treatment of Augustus himself: first, under the guise of Jupiter. In the great opening scene, Jupiter is accuser, sole witness, and judge over the offending Lycaon and has summarily executed his sentence before "consulting" his divine senate of yes-men. Again in the finale of the poem, which leads from the death and transfiguration of the divine Julius Caesar to the future apotheosis of his divine (adopted) son Augustus, Ovid declares that Caesar had to become a god so that Augustus would be the son of a god. Harmless enough, but he caps this bon mot by the epilogue which declares that his poetry will outlast the anger of Jupiter and all the forces of nature.

In fact, we do not know when Ovid began work on his *Metamorphoses*, epic in form but multigeneric in content. Although he claims it was unfinished when he was exiled, this polished text reflects many years of refining, and scholars reckon that he could have begun the new epic of world history as early as 2 BCE. He may have recited excerpts of his work in progress, but no one can say when it first found readers—to his contemporaries he was and had always been the poet of love.

As it is, his poetry of "bodies changed into new forms" absorbed some two hundred fifty tales into fifteen books, starting from creation itself and blending into an ostensibly chronological sequence transformation tales from Homer, Hesiod, Greek tragedy, Alexandrian catalog poets, and the explicit collections of "Transformations" by Nicander and Boios. But Ovid did not limit himself to retelling Greek stories: the last two books (14 and 15) include Italian and Roman transformation tales "up to my own time" with the apotheosis of Augustus' own "father" Julius Caesar a year before Ovid's birth. He built the episodes of book 14 around Virgil's epic, linking a sequence of transformations associated with Aeneas' journey from the Greek to the Italian world. In the full text of Homer's epics there is only one episode of humans transformed, when the witch Circe turns Odysseus' sailors into swine; this is reversed through the advice and magic herb provided to Odysseus by Hermes. We can read in full the mostly Euripidean tragedies which inspire Ovid's narrative versions and observe how often he adhered closely to key moments in the *Bacchae* or *Hecuba* or *Hippolytus*. So, too, when an Alexandrian text like Callimachus's *Hymn to Athena* or Apollonius's *Argonautica* has survived, readers of Ovid can hear the echo of his Greek model or recognize Ovid's transfer of a motif or image from one context—such as Athena's punishment of Tiresias for seeing her bathe—to another—Diana's terrible transformation of the unintended voyeur Actaeon.

But most of the evidence for Alexandrian metamorphosis narratives is fragmentary or second hand. The recent discovery of a papyrus from an alphabetical encyclopedia listing five metamorphoses beginning with the letter A, three of them from Hesiod's now lost *Catalogue of Women*, shows that tales of transformation were a recognized genre—and that women were the favorite victims of transformation in myth and verse—again, the transformation tales recorded in synopsis form by the second century CE Antoninus Liberalis include a dozen myths taken by Ovid from the *Heteroeoumena* (*Altered Bodies*) of Nicander (a near contemporary of Callimachus who wrote hexameter poetry) and a number from Boios' lost tales of bird metamorphosis. However, close comparison and reference to the mythological prose summaries of Apollodorus show that Ovid usually remodels the tradition to suit his own interpretation, changing names or facts or emphasis. Most of these myths were very old and had branched into variant narratives long before the Alexandrians; thus Ovid's poignant, extended tragic tale of the loving couple Ceyx and Alcyone changes not only details but also the psychology of the royal couple who, in earlier versions, provoked the gods by their boasting. In variant versions, Alcyone alone was transformed into the halcyon, and there was no deceptive dream of her drowned husband.

Jane Alison's main concern is Ovid's treatment of human experience in metamorphosis, often tales of love or desire involving pursuit and rape. She is surely right that Ovid's real theme is what E. A. Schmidt called *Poetische Menschenwelt*—suffering humanity. Thus, in the book's opening, the cosmogony, itself the biggest of all metamorphoses, leads into five tales of transformation, selected for their exceptional features—a sort of parade—before we follow Ovid into the more typical and better known tales of Callisto or Europa. These five tales report the fate of Lycaon; the transformation of the stones thrown by Deucalion and Pyrrha into a new race of mankind; the rescue of Daphne through transformation; and the victimization of Io, a sequence which includes a (fifth) embedded tale—Mercury's truncated tale of Syrinx, itself a doublet of Daphne's fate. How do they foreshadow Ovid's wider range of tales of love or, at least, desire?

Ovid's first narrative of erotic pursuit, introduced as "Apollo's first love" comes just after the flood, and it is a juvenile passion, inflicted on him by his kid brother Eros/Cupid, the adolescent god of love, with failure built in to the scenario. Cupid shoots a golden arrow to smite Apollo with desire for the nymph Daphne, but he also fires off a leaden arrow to make Daphne averse to courtship (as if such aversion was unnatural in a young woman and required an external cause!). The tone is comic, as Apollo breathlessly tries both to chase her and court her by boasting of his elite status. It is no comedy for Daphne, who runs from him desperately until her flight is stopped by the river who is also her father Peneus. For the first time in the poem transformation comes as an answer to an appeal for rescue, and it is described, bit by bit:

> A heavy paralysis possesses her limbs, her soft breast is enclosed in thin bark,
> her locks become foliage, her arms grow into branches, and her foot, once so
> swift, is held by sluggish roots, while a treetop takes over her face;
> only the gloss of beauty is retained.

Ovid's four lines provide a visual breakdown of the process changing the woman into a tree, which has appealed to ancient and more recent artists; from simple tomb reliefs in ancient Italy to the subtle and elegant works of Pollaiuolo and Bernini.

The tone of comedy is maintained for the longest tale in Ovid's first book, the sufferings and reward of Io (the first woman named in *Amores* 1.3). We can use two aspects of this ancient myth to illustrate Ovid's enormous talent: first, his learning. In the late fifth century BCE, Herodotus (I.1–4) began his history of intercontinental warfare with Io's abduction by Jupiter and transformation, cited by the Persians as the first cause for the enmity between Europe and Asia. For Ovid, she is the daughter of the river-god Inachus, but for Herodotus' Persian informants, she was the Argive King's daughter, kidnapped not by Jupiter but by Phoenician pirates. After Io, Ovid has Jupiter (not Phoenician pirates) abduct Europa, then follows Herodotus in listing the Greeks' abduction of Medea, then as the climax the Asian abduction of Helen. As Jupiter brought Io from Greece to Egypt, so disguised as a bull he brought the princess Europa to Greece from Phoenicia (see *Metamorphoses* 2); then Jason stole princess Medea from Colchis to Greece (cf. *Met.* 7); and finally, the Asian Paris prince of Troy stole Helen from Greece, bringing on the war and destruction of his city. Epics usually treated these acts not as physical rapes but as competition between communities to possess a talismanic symbol of power (almost a "trophy wife"). As in previous literature, Io was very much a victim, although she would become the benevolent goddess Isis. Catullus' friend Licinius Calvus honored her with a miniature epic, which, unfortunately, survived only in citations and allusions by both Ovid and Propertius. Twice Propertius addresses Io with sympathy as the first of women cruelly persecuted; 2.28.17–18, "Io, her face transformed, lowed in her early years: she is now a goddess who drank the waters of Nile as a cow." But for a different purpose he turns to condemning her at 2.33.5–14:

> The goddess who so often separated lovers, whoever she was, was always bitter. You too, Io, felt during the stealthy loves of Jupiter what it meant to embark on many journeys when he bid you—a girl—grow horns and waste your words on herds of cattle. Alas how often you scratched your face with branches of oak and chewed over in your stall the bushes you grazed on at pasture. Or is it that because Jupiter stripped that rustic look from your face that you became an arrogant goddess?

Calvus and Propertius clearly created their poetry out of the same empathy with the victim of metamorphosis which Ovid himself would develop so richly.

Ovid actually tells Io's tale in five acts, and our second approach to understanding his narrative concerns its theatricality. The most beloved form of theatrical performance in Rome from 23 BCE, the time of Ovid's young manhood, was the dance of pantomime artists, most famously Pylades and Bathyllus, from Greek Egypt and Asia Minor. Pantomime dancing would become a lasting craze in Rome and over her eastern empire. Just as Ovid himself claims in *Tristia* 2.519–20 that his poems were often danced (*sic!*) and gave pleasure to Augustus, so the language of his narratives, colored with highly suggestive details of posture and anatomical flexibility, reflects the influence of the brilliant pyrotechnics of Pylades or his pupils. The pantomime dancer did not sing; he wore masks with closed mouths, changing masks (but not his neutral and highly flexible robe or stole) as he enacted different roles in a mythical tale, sometimes alternating roles within a single scene. It was left to his body to convey all the character's sufferings and emotions. So if we joined Ovid's audience of readers, he would suggest to them a pantomime dancer's scenario and adaptation of the tale of Io. In the first scene (588–600), Jupiter accosts her as she is walking home through the forest. Like Daphne, she tries to run away, but he overtakes her and engulfs her in mist. In the second scene (601–623), panicked by the jealous suspicions of Juno, he transforms the woman he has not yet had time to rape into a cow. Juno demands the gleaming cow as a gift and sets the thousand-eyed Argos to watch over her. In the third scene (624–667), Ovid combines visual and verbal descriptive language borrowed from Licinius Calvus: his Io grazes on bitter grass and lies on the bare earth drinking muddy streams (632–34). There is even a recognition scene: seeing the reflection of her new horns in the water—changed beyond visual recognition by her doting father Inachus—Io is just able to scratch her name with her hoof, provoking his incongruous lament that he must now seek not a prince but a steer among his flocks for a son-in-law. The watch-monster Argos will not let her rest until (scene 4.668–719) Jupiter sends Mercury to distract him. Mercury's method is to send Argos to sleep by telling a tedious and slow-moving tale of Pan's failed rape of Syrinx, an unmistakable clone of Apollo's pursuit of Daphne. When Mercury kills Argos, Juno in revenge sends a dreadful Erinys (in other versions a gadfly) to drive Io ever onward, until she sinks to the ground and rearing her neck backward to raise her face, "the only part of her she could raise," she laments to Jupiter with groaning and tears and mournful mooing (732). This precipitates the denouement when Jupiter hears her appeal and succeeds in persuading Juno to forgive him and Io, leading to a reverse metamorphosis, the only one Ovid will offer in detail.

> The bristles flee her body
> Her horns contract, her gaping eyeballs narrow
> Her huge mouth shrinks, shoulders and arms return,
> Her hoof dissolves into five fingernails,
> Nothing remains except the cow's creamy color,
> The girl stands upright, content with just two feet
> But dreads to speak, fearing a cowlike moo,
> Timidly testing interrupted speech.

A one-line epilogue brings us to the Augustan present: Io is now a goddess, worshipped by thronging crowds clad in linen.

In the sheer verbal virtuosity of Ovid's narratives, many details are intensely visual, almost compelling his audience to see the actions and sufferings of his central figures. The virtuoso pantomime dancers had only recently come to Rome when Ovid was first composing, and scholars prompted by the relative lack of textual evidence have only recently turned their attention to the nonverbal art of the pantomime, the quasi-balletic form in which a single brilliant dancer silently swayed and undulated his body to represent phases of a drama. We can profit now from one all-important collection: Edith Hall and Rosie Wyles' *New Directions in Ancient Pantomime* (Oxford 2008) in which readers should consult not only Hall's comprehensive introduction but also Ingleheart's paper specifically on Ovid and pantomime, "Et mea sunt populo saltata poemata saepe" (Tristia 2.519). Two contributors to that collection have also published valuable books and articles: Ismene Lada Richards "*Mutata corpora; Ovid's*

Changing Forms and the Metamorphic Bodies of Pantomime Dancing" (Transactions of the American Philological Association, 2013 vol. 143), 105–152; and Ruth Webb, "Inside the Mask: Pantomime from the Performer's Perspective," 43–60 in Hall and Wyles, and her monograph *Demons and Dancers* (Harvard University Press, 2008).

When the exiled Ovid composed the defense of his erotic poetry (*Tristia* 2), he insists that Augustus himself enjoyed the theater, both pantomimes and the more ribald mime. He also claims that Virgil's poetry (probably the *Eclogues*) and his own poems were often performed on stage. For other pantomime themes, it is worth consulting the second-century Lucian's dialogue *On the Dance,* which lists a large number of themes from Greek myths and tragedies (§§ 40–63), now accessible to the Augustan public, even outside Rome and the great cities of Asia, through the *Metamorphoses.*

The solo dancer was a star everywhere, famous and wealthy: it was he who financed and controlled his (usually) one-man program and could take on each role of a drama in turn, changing his close-lipped mask but not his basic costume between roles. It is clear from Lucian's dialogue *On the Dance* that dancers in the age of Augustus took many scenarios from Ovid, but we should also allow for Ovid himself basing details of his narrative on remembered performances: the process works in both directions. If dance steps and postures were symbolic, they could be used to convey a metamorphosis such as that of Actaeon even without the accompaniment of narrative libretti. Thanks to Jane Alison's gifts as both poet and novelist, modern readers can experience in her subtle and stirring translations the expert Augustan readers' response to Ovid's narratives told in language that stimulates their visual fantasy and lets them share his characters' rare joys, and mental and physical pain.

Plate I: *"My poems have often been danced for a crowd"* —Ovid, *Tristia* 2.519 (Roman mosaic, 3rd CE)

Plate II: *"So your man will be at the dinner party, too. I wish it were his last supper"*
—*Am.* 1.4 (Roman mosaic, 2nd CE)

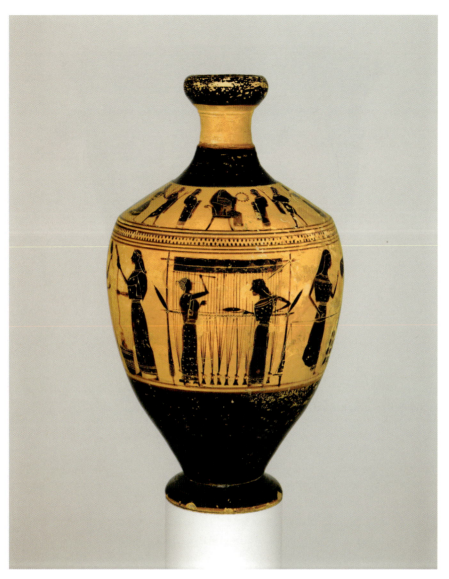

Plate III: *"The two set up in separate stations and stretch fine threads upon twinned looms"*
—*Arachne* (black-figure lekythos, 550–530 BCE)

Plate IV: *"They cluster upon him, muzzles deep in his flesh, and tear apart their master"*
—*Actaeon* (red-figure bell crater, about c. 470 BCE)

Plate V: *"While she and the snakes were deeply asleep he swiped the head from her neck . . ."*
Perseus and Andromeda (and Medusa) (red-figure pelike, 475–425 BCE)

Plate VI: *"He was so entranced by the image he saw that he almost forgot to keep beating his wings"* —*Perseus and Andromeda (and Medusa)* (fresco, last decade of 1st BCE)

Plate VII: *"She clutches his horn with one hand and his back with the other. Her shivering veils flit in the wind . . ."* —*Europa* (marble, early mid-2nd CE)

Plate VIII: *"She just bathed her lovely self in her pond, often drew a boxwood comb through her hair, and gazed in her glassy pool to see what looked best"* —*Salmacis* (red-figure amphora, 6th BCE)

Plate IX: *"Dis controlled his temper no more: he spurred the frothing horses, swung his royal scepter, and plunged it deep in the pool's sunken bed"* —*Proserpina* (marble sarcophagus, c. 140–150 CE)

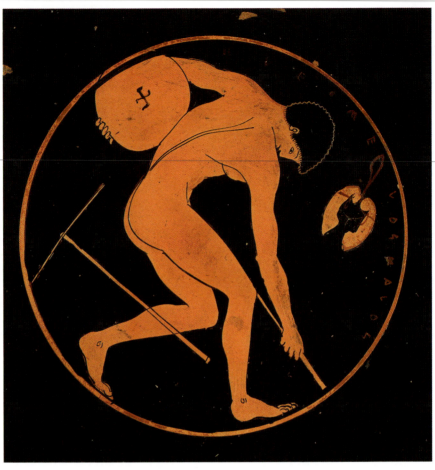

Plate X: *"The two stripped off their clothes, slicked their skin with sleek olive oil, and set off to compete with the discus"* —Hyacinth (red-figure cup, 5th BCE)

Plate XI: *"I won't be had unless beaten in a race. So race with me"* —*Atalanta* (mosaic, late 3rd or early 4th CE)

Plate XII: *"Adonis pierced the boar with a slanting thrust"* —Adonis (red figure cup, 500–475 BCE)

Plate XIII: *"I used to be human but, it's true, addicted to ocean, for my work was with the sea"*
—*Glaucus* (red-figure cup, 510–500 BCE)

Plate XIV: *"She stands amid raving dogs that were once her poor hips"* —*Scylla* (terracotta relief, 5th BCE)

Plate XV: *"'If alive I offend the living and dead I offend the dead, throw me from both zones: / change me.'"* —*Myrrha* (terracotta, 3rd BCE)

Plate XVI: *"In greening woods one day he'd seen a pair of snakes entwined and struck them with his walking-stick—then changed from man to woman"* —Tiresias (bronze, forming handle of drawer or door, Roman)

CHANGE ME

Introduction

SEXUALITY AND GENDER IN CLASSICAL ANTIQUITY
Alison Keith

In classical antiquity, sexual relations and gender norms were defined not on the basis of object preference but on sociopolitical status.[1] Elite male citizens, who authored the overwhelming majority of our extant ancient textual material (whether literary or documentary), enjoyed privileged access to the bodies of their social inferiors, both male and female. By contrast, upper-class women were sexually available only within a socially sanctioned union of legitimate marriage with a man from their own elite social circle. In both ancient Athens and classical Rome, moreover, the goal of marriage was explicitly articulated as the production of legitimate children for the inheritance of paternal ancestral property. For their sexual pleasure, elite men could turn to slaves, prostitutes, and the socially disenfranchised (such as the young, the poor, freedmen and freedwomen, resident aliens, and foreigners). An Athenian politician famously summarized the array of female sexual partners available to his male peers in democratic Athens with the following statement ([Dem.] 59.122): "We keep courtesans [*hetairas*, lit. "female companions"] to give us pleasure, concubines [*pallakai*] to tend our person on a daily basis, and wives [*gunaikai*] to produce legitimate children for us and be trustworthy guardians of our possessions." He does not include male objects of desire in this list, but there is abundant evidence of same-sex sexual relationships, both male and female, in the literature of classical antiquity, with the lyric poetry of Sappho (*fl.* second half of the seventh century BCE) long considered the *locus classicus* of female homoeroticism and the philosophical dialogues of Plato (c. 429–347 BCE) that of male.[2]

Explicit literary treatment of sex at Rome begins a generation before Ovid with the poet Catullus (c. 84–54 BCE) and his friends, who developed a fresh way of writing about sexuality and gender in Latin, influenced by the lyric poetry of ancient Greece, especially that of Sappho and Callimachus (*fl.* 285–240 BCE). Catullus wrote love lyrics celebrating the beauty and wit of a "girl" (*puella*) or "mistress" (*domina*) whom he calls Lesbia, a name apparently chosen with reference to Sappho's birthplace on the island of Lesbos. He also wrote love lyrics to a youth whom he names Juventius, a Roman gentilician (family name) derived from the Latin word for "young man," *iuuenis*. Later Latin authors retained Catullus' terminology for a man's mistress (much of it already in use in early Roman comedy of the late third and early second centuries BCE) and employed the term *puer* (boy), occasionally in combination with the adjective *delicatus* (pretty), to denote a male object of amatory desire. While the mistress's sexual appeal could last from puberty through her childbearing years (though childbearing itself was not considered flattering to the figure—discussed later),[3] that of the *puer delicatus* was more fleeting, lasting only from early adolescence through the first flush of hormonal changes and ending abruptly with the onset of adult male secondary sexual characteristics such as beard and body hair. The Romans, like the Greeks, viewed erotic desire for women and boys as both natural and interchangeable—a matter of taste requiring the observation of certain social rules, primarily with respect to class-appropriate object choices (e.g., marriage with, rather than rape of, citizen women).

This attitude was reinforced by the model of dominance and submission that articulated not only sexual relationships but also the gender hierarchy in classical antiquity. In our extant corpus of classical texts and material evidence, both Greeks and Romans conceptualize sexual relations as "naturally" involving an adult citizen man (like themselves),[4] who actively "penetrates" the other party, construed as a sexually "passive" other (woman, boy, or slave), who was thereby reduced to a feminized status.[5] This paradigm of sexual relations between active citizen male and passive feminized other maps easily on to the sociopolitical codes and conventions of gender relations in ancient Greece and Rome, where adult citizen men exercised social and political authority over women, children, slaves, and foreigners. For this reason the Romans, unlike the Greeks, never came to regard erotic relationships between adult citizen males and adolescent citizen boys as honorable and commendable (as they appear in, e.g., Plato's *Phaedrus* and *Symposium*), and some of the most vitriolic abuse in Roman literature is reserved for male-male sexual relations (discussed later, on Cat. 16).[6]

This is not to suggest, however, that male–male affective relations were not central to both Roman society and Latin literature. In a poem addressed to his friend and fellow poet the Roman politician Licinius Calvus, Catullus employs the language of love in a description of competitive verse composition (Cat. 50.1–17):

> Yesterday, Licinius, at our leisure
> we sported much in my tablets,
> as we had agreed to be self-indulgent [*delicatos*]:
> each of us, writing little verses,
> was playing now with this metre, now with that one,

going back and forth in turn over jokes and wine.
And I went away from there, Licinius,
fired by your charm and eloquence,
so that neither could food please me in my wretched state,
nor sleep cover my poor eyes in repose,
but, overcome with passion, I tossed and turned
over the whole bed, desiring to see daylight
in order to speak with you and be with you.
But after my limbs, tired out from thrashing around,
lay half-dead on the little bed,
I composed this poem for you, my charming friend,
from which you might see my suffering . . .[7]

Poetic composition is here figured as both emulative and erotic, with the exchange of verses cementing the homosocial bonds of privilege, poetry, and desire that unite Catullus and Calvus in friendship.[8] Catullus addresses some of his most passionate lyric and elegiac poetry to Lesbia (Cat. 5, 7, 51, 72, 75, 107) and Juventius (Cat. 24, 48, 81, 99), but he sets these poems in collections dedicated to Cornelius Nepos (Cat. 1) and Hortensius Hortalus (Cat. 65), thereby subsuming his *puella* and *puer delicatus* into gifts presented to his male literary patrons. Within the collections, moreover, Lesbia and Juventius circulate between Catullus and his friends and rivals—Furius (Cat. 11, 16, 23), Aurelius (Cat. 11, 15, 16, 21), Fabullus (Cat. 13), Calvus (Cat. 50), and Caelius (Cat. 58). The circulation of Lesbia (the name encompassing both Catullus' mistress and his erotic verse) among Catullus and his friends, however, discredits her even as it wins the poet fame. In a poem to Caelius, for example, Catullus characterizes Lesbia as sexually promiscuous despite his unique love for her (Cat. 58):

Caelius—our Lesbia, that Lesbia,
that famous Lesbia, whom Catullus loved alone,
more than himself and all his relatives,
now on street-corners and in back-alleys
peels the great-hearted grandsons of Remus.

In Catullus' brutally frank verses, Lesbia is reduced to a cheap whore, plying her trade on the streets. Yet, coming as it does at the end of the lyric collection, this short poem can be interpreted as the literalization of a literary trope that figures the publication of amatory poetry as the mistress's sexual circulation among men. Catullus' poetry, like Ovid's a generation later, circulated among the Roman political elites within a culture of institutionalized social relations that consolidated male authority in and through the bodies of women, slaves, and foreigners. The feminine clichés to which Catullus' portrait of Lesbia appeals not only strengthened male social bonds and elite authority (over female, foreigner, and slave) but also naturalized the hierarchy of the sexes—as also the rule of the Roman elites over other nations and classes—on display in Latin literature and Roman culture. Catullan verse thus made explicit the poet's participation in the elite male homosocial network central to Latin political, rhetorical, and literary culture.

Among the most exciting aspects of the poems of Catullus and his friends were their topicality (in naming both well-known contemporaries and notorious scandals of the day) and, especially, their sexiness (in exploring erotic pleasure, exposure, and risk). Catullus' famous sparrow poems offer charming evidence of the latter feature of his verse (Cat. 2):

> Sparrow, my girl's pet—
> she often plays with you, often holds you in her lap,
> often gives you, eagerly seeking it, her forefinger
> and often provokes keen nibbles from you,
> whenever, bright-eyed with longing for me,
> she takes pleasure in making some joke,
> a little solace for her grief, I think,
> so that her intense passion may subside:
> I wish I could play with you as she does
> and relieve my mind's sad cares.
> So pleasing is it to me as they say
> the little golden apple was to the swift girl
> that loosed her long-bound girdle.

The scholarly debate about whether the Latin word for sparrow, *passer*, is slang for "penis" (on the model of the Greek word for sparrow, *strouthos*, which gave its name to the huge phallus of Roman mime, *stroutheum*) to some extent misses the point of this sexy little poem, in which the antics of the girl's pet offer an erotically suggestive model for the lovers' play.[9] Whether or not the poet-lover's penis can be seen in all the details of the bird's activities with the girl, her pet's privileged access to her erogenous zones can hardly be denied. The poem that follows, moreover, seems to lament the "little death" of sexual union (whether in impotence or orgasm, Cat. 3):

> Mourn, o Venuses and Cupids,
> and as many more charming fellows as there are:

my girl's sparrow has died,
the sparrow, my girl's pet,
whom she loved more than her own eyes.
For he was honey-sweet, and knew his own mistress
as well as a girl knows her mother;
nor did he often move from her lap,
but hopping around, now here now there,
he was always chirping to his mistress alone:
now he's going on that shadowy journey
from which, they say, no one returns.
But may it go ill with you, evil shades
of Orcus who swallow all pretty things:
such a pretty sparrow you've stolen from me.
O badly done! O poor little sparrow!
Now because of you, my girl's
darling eyes are a little swollen and red from weeping.

The poem's humor is evident in the mock-serious invocation of multiple Venuses, Cupids, and sexual sophisticates (1–2), as well as in the imprecation of Hell's shades; and it continues in the treatment of the death of the girl's pet with full funerary honors. The poet's teasing touch here can be paralleled in Hellenistic Greek epigrams lamenting the death of pets as coded double-entendres for the "death" of the speaker's erection. But this fresh and engaging little poem, and the many others like it composed by Catullus and his friends, seems to have burst upon the wider Latin literary scene with a shocking audacity that offended readers who subscribed to a stricter Roman standard of morality.[10] In fact, Catullus advises Lesbia to ignore the gossip of "rather severe old men" and the threat of the evil eye in his famous kiss poems (Cat. 5, 7), even as he treats his friends' amatory escapades as juicy material for his racy verse (Cat. 6, 10).

Catullus himself vociferously denies that his sexy poetry reflects his own sexual practice in some of the most sexually aggressive language that survives from classical antiquity (Cat. 16):

I'll fuck you in your ass and mouth,
Aurelius you queer and you catamite Furius!
You thought from my little verses,
because they're a little soft, that I'm without shame.
For while it's proper for a right-thinking poet to be chaste
himself, there's no need at all for his verses to be;
indeed they have wit and charm

if they're a little soft and shameless,
and can provoke some itch,
I'm not saying in boys [*pueris*], but in these hairy guys
who can't move their stiff groins.
But you, because you counted many thousands of kisses,
did you think I was a fag?
I'll fuck you in your ass and mouth.

To modern readers unfamiliar with the codes and conventions of ancient sexuality, it can seem that the very poem in which Catullus denies queer sexual practices actually espouses them, with his male addressees and threats of same-sex rape (anal and oral). But if we recall the "penetration" model of sexual relations discussed previously, we can see that in fact this poem confirms, rather than subverts, Catullus' adult male privileges and thereby ratifies his masculinity rather than unmanning him. For the poet threatens to inflict on his critics' bodies an array of sexually penetrative acts that conform very precisely to the privileged model of sexual penetration that belonged exclusively to the elite citizen male in ancient Rome and feminized the unfortunate targets of his aggressively masculine sexuality.

Catullus died a decade before Ovid's birth in 43 BCE, and the intervening decade saw the end of the republican form of Rome's government in the civil wars begun by Caesar and continued by his heir Octavian, later known as Augustus, who established a monarchical form of government at Rome after the Battle of Actium in 31 BCE. Augustus' policy of moral and religious reform had to wait until he had secured full military control of Rome's Mediterranean empire, but by the 20s BCE he was in a position to promote marriage and reproduction amongst the Roman upper classes, whose numbers had been sharply reduced by two decades of civil war. Poems composed by Horace and Propertius in this decade bear witness to the *princeps'* exertion of social, if not legal, pressure on the Roman elite to marry and produce children. In an elegy usually dated to the mid-20s BCE, Propertius celebrates with his mistress Cynthia the withdrawal of a law that would have separated them, apparently by requiring the poet to marry within his own station and sire sons for the Roman army (Prop. 2.7):[11]

Cynthia, you rejoiced at the withdrawal of the law, over which
        we wept—each of us for a long time—upon its proclamation,
lest it separate us: though not Jupiter himself
        could separate two lovers against their will.
"But Caesar is great." But Caesar is great under arms:
        conquered nations have no power in love.
For sooner would I suffer this head to leave my neck,

than could I waste torches at a bride's behest,
or, as a married man, pass by your shuttered doorstep,
  looking back at its betrayal with my wet eyes.
Ah! What kind of sleep could my pipe serenade for you—
  pipe, more savage than the funeral trumpet!
Why should I give sons to the triumphs of our country?
  No soldier will come from my blood.
But if I were to accompany the camp of my girl (the only real camp in my
  view),
  Castor's horse wouldn't be great enough for me to travel on.
For there my glory has earned a great name—
  a glory reaching all the way to those living at the cold Dnieper.
You alone please me: let me alone please you, Cynthia!
  This love will be worth more even than my father's bloodline.

In a slightly later ode, Horace denounces the irresponsible pleasure mongering espoused by Propertius and links upper-class adulteries to the neglect of Roman religion (Hor. *Odes* 3.6.1–8, 17–32, 45–48):

You will pay undeservedly for the crimes of our ancestors,
Roman [man], until you have rebuilt the temples
  and collapsing shrines of the gods,
    and the statues foul with black smoke.
You rule because you keep yourself subordinate to the gods.
From this principle carry out every beginning, to this refer the end:
  the gods, neglected, have given many
    ills to the grieving West.
Generations fertile in crime first stained
marriage, lineage, and homes:
  derived from this source, disaster
    flowed into the fatherland and among the populace.
The teenage girl enjoys being taught
Ionian dances, is instructed in skills,
  and now even contemplates
    illicit love affairs wholeheartedly.
Soon she seeks younger adulterers
at her husband's parties, nor waits to choose
  the man to whom to give unpermitted joys
    in secret when the lights have been removed,
but openly rises at a man's bidding, in the full
knowledge of her husband, whether a shopkeeper

> invites her, or the captain of a Spanish ship,
>> an expensive buyer of disgrace.
> What has the damaging present-day not diminished?
> The time of our parents, worse than that of our grandparents,
>> has borne us, still worse, and soon to produce
>> an even more vicious progeny.

Both poems have been interpreted as evidence of an interest on the part of Augustus, already in the mid-20s BCE, in legislating the restoration of Roman religion and/or the renewal of Roman sexual morality. Some years later Augustus succeeded in the latter goal, authoring two sets of laws about marriage, reproduction, and sexuality in 18 BCE, the year before he celebrated the Secular Games, which claimed to initiate a newly purified generation of Romans, cleansed of the taint of civil war (and for which Horace produced the cult hymn sung by matched choirs of youths and maidens).

The two Julian laws (so-called from Augustus' gentilician Julius, assumed on the occasion of the death of his great-uncle Caesar, who adopted him in his will) promoted marriage and childbearing and criminalized adultery among the upper classes.[12] The *lex Iulia de maritandis ordinibus* imposed penalties on senatorial and equestrian men and women who were unmarried in their childbearing years and awarded benefits to the parents of three or more children (for men, preferential career advancement; for women, exemption from financial oversight). The *lex Iulia de adulteriis coercendis* made sexual relations with a married woman a state crime to be tried before a standing criminal court, requiring a woman's husband to divorce her if he even suspected her of sexual infidelity and imposing civil disabilities on convicted adulterers. The unpopularity of the laws (implied, even before their promulgation, in the poems of Propertius and Horace quoted previously) was such that the marriage and reproductive legislation had to be supplemented a generation later in the *lex Papia Poppaea* of 9 CE, sponsored by the two consuls of the year, both childless bachelors.

It was in this period of perceived sexual license and concomitant pressure for moral renewal in the 20s BCE that Ovid came of age and started composing poetry. His earliest verse, for Corinna "so-called under a false name," he says he first performed publicly when his beard had been cut once or twice, perhaps between the ages of fifteen and eighteen in 28–25 BCE. These poems, later collected into several books of *Amores* (*Loves*), made him famous at an early age as an amatory poet, and all his subsequent work bears the stamp of pleasure in, and knowledge of, the appetites of the flesh. The epigram that prefaces Ovid's *Amores* draws programmatic attention to the sensual delight that awaits the reader of his first collection (*Am. Epigr.*):

> We who were only recently five little books by Naso, are now three; their author preferred this work to the former: though you may now take no pleasure [*uoluptas*] in having read us, the penalty will be the lighter with two books removed.

The Latin *uoluptas*, from which we derive the English term "voluptuary" (used of a person devoted to luxury and sensual pleasure), refers to any of the pleasures of the senses but can also mean, quite specifically, "sexual pleasure" (as it does, for example, in *Amores* 1.4.47). The sexual valence seems especially suitable as an introduction to *Amores* 1.4 and 1.5, Ovid's highly erotic descriptions of a Roman dinner party and an afternoon siesta, respectively (both included in this selection). At a dinner party, Ovid suggests, there are plenty of opportunities for sexual touching, with the lovers drinking from one another's glasses and nibbling one another's food, embracing one another, exchanging kisses, playing footsie, and even engaging in hurried sex (*properata uoluptas*) beneath their cloaks. In 1.4, therefore, Ovid entreats his mistress *not* to indulge, with her official lover, in all the pleasurable canoodling he's taught her and which he puts on display in the afternoon tryst described in 1.5. The covert climax ("that sweet melting end") of 1.4 is laid open to view in 1.5, with Corinna's named entry into the collection. No "nervous girl," Corinna is easily stripped of her scanty dress, as Ovid bares her physical charms to the reader.

   Ovid's erotic lexicon, though elevated in tone (as is appropriate to the genres of epic and elegy in which he worked), is far more physically explicit in the *Amores* than in the elegiac poetry of his contemporaries, Propertius and Tibullus. The first-century CE Roman critic and educator Quintilian draws attention to this feature of Ovidian verse in his discussion of the Roman elegists (*Inst. Or.* 10.1.93):

> In elegy too, we compete with the Greeks. In this genre, the author Tibullus seems to me especially polished and refined. There are those who prefer Propertius. Ovid is more risqué [*lasciuior*] than either of them, just as Gallus is harsher.

Quintilian characterizes Ovid very astutely here, for the adjective he employs, a comparative form of *lasciuus*, from which the English term "lascivious" is derived, also means "free from restraint in sexual matters" (*OLD* s.v. 4), and well captures the frank sexuality of Ovid's elegiac verse. Indeed, after the implied promise of sexual pleasure in the prefatory epigram to the *Amores*, Ovid opens the collection proper with a poem that sexualizes the very movement of the elegiac couplet (1.1.27): "Let my work swell in six measures, settle back in five." The hint of tumescence and deflation in the regular alternation of the expansive hexameter with the shorter pentameter is nicely calculated to suggest the poet-speaker's carnal approach to love throughout the collection.

Although the Ovidian poet-lover occasionally encounters setbacks in his amatory affairs (e.g., in 1.8 where his mistress's bawd advises her not to encourage poets as lovers because they don't give expensive presents, and in 1.12 where his girlfriend declines a date), he is more often successful in his erotic dealings, even if (or perhaps because!) he is not always faithful to his mistress. In 2.4, for example, Ovid acknowledges a hundred reasons why he's always in love and claims his love is ready to canvass (literally, "go round") all the girls. In the paired poems *Amores* 2.7 and 2.8, moreover, he shows himself playing the field: addressing 2.7 to Corinna, who has accused him of having sex with her maid Cypassis, he denies any interest in a low-born paramour; addressing 2.8 to Cypassis, he wonders what gave his double-game away and threatens to reveal "how many times and in what positions" they've had sex, if she won't sleep with him again that very day. In 2.10, he even boasts of his sexual prowess in the service of two (unnamed) women and hopes to die *in flagrante* (2.10.23–30, 35–38):

I'm up for the job: my limbs are slender, not without strength;
> my body lacks weight, not potency.
Sexual intercourse [*uoluptas*] will stimulate my flank to vigor:
> no girl has been disappointed by my work in bed;
often I've devoted the whole night to sex,
> and I was still ready, with a strong body, in the morning.
Happy the man whom Venus' sport destroys in mutual pleasure!
> May the gods make this the cause of my death! . . .
Let it be my lot to flag in Venus' activity,
> and when I die let me be released in the very midst of the job;
and let someone, weeping at my funeral, say
> "This death of yours was worthy of your life."

Ovid's parody of the soldier's desire for a heroic death in war continues in the poet-lover's announcement of his erotic triumph in 2.12 (included in this selection): "Set the laurels of triumph up there on my head: / I've won! Corinna's here in my lap."

More surprising, indeed absolutely shocking, are the two poems that follow his erotic triumph, describing the results of the *amator*'s sexual potency for Corinna—a life-threatening abortion (2.13.1–2): "While she rashly attacks the burden of her heavy womb, / Corinna lies ill, in doubt of her life." The only reason the poet-lover can imagine for an abortion is her desire "for her belly to lack the crime of wrinkles" (2.14.7). Recent scholarship, however, has drawn attention to the economic and physical hardship female sex-workers faced before reliable contraception was available,[13] not only from the loss of income while pregnant and nursing but also from the violence of abortion, which Ovid describes so forcefully here (2.14.27): "why do you subject your vitals to weapons and dig out their contents?"

It is also jarring to turn from Ovid's discussion of Corinna's self-inflicted abortion in 2.13 and 2.14, to his light-hearted poem addressed to the signet ring that he plans to send to his girlfriend in 2.15. This elegy shows him early at work on the theme of metamorphosis, in a highly erotic context, as he wishes to become his own gift so that he can touch his mistress beneath her clothes and enjoy her "kisses" when she seals letters (2.15.9–14, 25–26):

> Oh! I wish I could suddenly be turned into my own gift
>   by the arts of Medea or Proteus!
> Then, when I want to touch my mistress's breasts
>   and put my left hand under her shift,
> I would slip from her finger, though a narrow circlet and tight,
>   and fall loose into her lap with wonderful skill! . . .
> But, I suppose, once I see you naked my penis will swell with lust [*libidine surgent*]
>   and, in the form of a ring, I will play the role of a man.

His potency even as a ring is consistent with his libidinous self-representation throughout the collection, even on the occasion of his unexpected impotence in 3.7. Like the pair of abortion poems, this elegy has often been censured for a theme unsuited to the decorum of elegiac verse, but it coheres closely with the carnal sexuality on display in the *Amores* (3.7.1–15, 23–26):

> But I suppose the girl wasn't beautiful, well groomed,
>   or often longed for in my prayers?
> Nonetheless, I held her to no purpose, unhappily limp,
>   and lay a criminal burden on an idle bed;
> nor could I use the pleasurable part of my feeble groin,
>   though I desired to and she wanted it just as much.
> Indeed, she put her ivory arms,
>   fairer than Thracian snow, round my neck,
> thrust wanton kisses in my mouth with eager tongue,
>   and sexily laid her leg beneath mine;
> she whispered seductively, called me master,
>   and said all the well-known words that help besides.
> But my limbs, as if drugged by cold hemlock, were sluggish
>   and failed the task at hand.
> I lay an idle trunk, all show and useless weight . . .

But only recently I did blond Chlide twice in succession, fair Pitho three
    times,
      and serviced Libas, too, three times with my attentions;
I remember Corinna demanding from me—and me supplying—
      nine times in succession in one short night!

The Ovidian speaker's unabashed celebration of his erstwhile sexual prowess
is unparalleled in Latin elegy (though not in Catullan lyric, where Catullus
promises a girl nine fucks in succession one afternoon, Cat. 32). Equally unpar-
alleled is the Ovidian speaker's frank admission of sexual failure (3.7.63–80):

What joys didn't I conceive in my silent mind,
    what sexual positions didn't I imagine and arrange!
But my limbs lay as if already dead,
    more shamefully drooping than yesterday's rose,
which now—look!—revive and grow strong out of season,
    and now demand their work and military service.
Why don't you lie down there modestly, worst part of myself?
    I've been caught before by your promises!
You deceive your master—through you I was caught unarmed
    and bore sad reverses to my great shame.
My girl didn't even disdain to move
    her hand here and touch me gently.
But after she saw my penis unable to rise with any tricks
    and forgetful of her, she said
"Why are you toying with me? Who asked you, madman,
    to lay your limbs in my bed uninvited?
Either a Colchian poisoner has cursed you by piercing a woolen figure
    or you're coming to me exhausted from another love affair."

Just as the mistress's promiscuity can be interpreted on a literary level, so here
the poet's impotence may have symbolic import, playing an important role in
articulating the final book's program of disengagement from elegy in the *Amores*.
Despite the blandishments of a compliant elegiac mistress, the lover proves im-
potent in a metaphorical enactment of the poet's flagging interest in elegiac com-
position. Thus the speaker's body, formerly well-endowed for erotic encounters,
as he boasts, is now adapted to the task of elegiac closure and so is figured as "an
idle trunk, all show and useless weight."
    While the elegiac girlfriends featured in the *Amores* are consistently char-
acterized as beautiful, learned, and lascivious, seductive flatterers who know
how to dress their hair to advantage and clothe themselves in robes of exquisite

delicacy, by the third book the speaker has tired of their caprice. Although he counsels his mistress's official lover not to guard her too closely in 3.4, his very success in love (and love poetry!) has advertised her charms so widely that he has, in effect, prostituted her. (We see here the recurrence of the literary trope that figures the success of the poet's erotic verse as his mistress's sexual circulation among men.) Thus he observes bitterly (3.8.5–6): "although my little books pleased my mistress beautifully, / where my books can go, I can't." He complains that she shuts the door to him in order to admit a wealthy man of equestrian rank (3.8.9–10). But he cavils at being cuckolded (3.11.25–26): "I'm told she's ill: I bolt to her house, rushing with love; / I get there; she's not sick for *him*." Ovid takes some responsibility for her public notoriety (3.12.5–12):

> The girl who's supposed to be mine to love, mine *alone*,   5
>   I dread is now open to all.
> Am I wrong, or did my own books make her famous?
>   Yes: she's on sale thanks to my talent.
> I deserve it. What made me broadcast her beauty?
>   My fault the girl's on the market.   10
> I've pimped her delights; torched the way for a lover;
>   my hands have flung open her door.

Ovid here both accuses his mistress of prostitution and accepts a measure of responsibility for her circulation among men. Moreover, his placement of the poem so close to the end of the *Amores* as a whole, invites interpretation in metaliterary terms, as a meditation on the circulation of "Corinna" (both his girlfriend and his poetry about her) among the Roman reading public.

Throughout the *Amores*, as later in the *Art of Love* and even in the exile poetry, Ovid delights in the fame his poems have won him (if not that which has accrued to his mistress). Already in the *Amores,* he jokes of knowing someone who claims to be Corinna (2.17.29), though he elsewhere reports contemporary speculation denying her very existence (*Ars* 3.538). In *Amores* 2.18, moreover, he mentions his two other celebrated elegiac collections, the *Heroides* (poetic epistles from mythological heroines to their absent and/or unfaithful lovers) and the *Art of Love* (an erotic treatise in three books, with the first two addressed to men, detailing how to find a girl, win her, and keep her; and a third, supplementary book about female deportment and makeup, addressed to women). Ovid predicates his posture as a teacher of love (*praeceptor amoris*) in the *Art of Love* on his amatory "experience" in the *Amores* (*Ars* 1.29), and modern critics have noted that, as in the *Amores*, men are the chief beneficiaries of his instructions, even in the third book, which is ostensibly addressed to women.

Like the *Amores*, the *Art of Love* is extraordinarily frank on the subject of sexuality. As the poet-*praeceptor* notes (*Ars* 1.453), "'This is the toil, this is the task': to get laid without paying first." This cheeky statement of his didactic project is particularly outrageous in its adaptation of the Vergilian Sibyl's portentous words to Aeneas (*Aen.* 6.126–129):

"Trojan son of Anchises, the descent to Avernus is easy:
night and day the door of black Dis stands open;
but to retrace your steps and walk out to the upper air—
this is the toil, this is the task."

No wonder Augustus wasn't pleased with Ovid, subverting the heroic mission of Vergil's Aeneas to the salacious, newly criminalized project of amatory seduction! But Ovid was careful to warn wellborn matrons away from his verse, right from the start (*Ars* 1.31–34):

Keep your distance, slender fillets, chastity's mark,
      and you who conceal your feet with a long flounce:
we sing of safe love, clandestine affaires that are allowed,
      and there will be no crime in my poem.

These are the marks of a respectable woman's dress: woolen fillets for the hair, and a long robe that reaches the feet (the *stola*, worn by rich, married women at Rome) with a band sewn along the edge. In this way, he warns off freeborn, especially upper class, women whose marriages and reproductive capacity Augustus was most concerned to regulate in the Julian laws of 18 BCE.

But his repeated warnings must also have incited some to read further. Thus, the warning at the beginning of the third book implicitly invites those with a prurient curiosity to read on (3.23–27):

Virtue herself is also a woman in dress and name:
      it's no wonder if she pleases her people (i.e., the virtuous Romans).
But such minds are not demanded by our *Art*;
      our smaller sails suit my little craft.
Nothing except sexy love-affairs [*lasciui amores*] are learned through me.

The risqué affairs Ovid promises here must be supposed to be those with slaves and freedwomen, rather than with respectable married women, and so he states explicitly toward the end of the book (3.611–616):

I was going to pass over how to elude
    a husband or a watchful guardian.
Let the bride fear her husband, let the guardianship of a bride be fixed;
    this is seemly, this the laws and right and modesty command.
But who could bear that you too be watched, whom the praetor's rod has
    recently
    redeemed (from slavery)? Come to my rites, so as to learn how to deceive!

But his warning comes far too late—we're nearly finished the book and surely this is the best part! Indeed, Ovid does not hesitate to offer explicit instruction in sex, to both men (2.703–732) and women (3.769–788, 798–804). The poet-*praeceptor* even explains his own sexual preferences (2.683–698):

I hate sex that doesn't release both parties:
    this is why I'm less moved by love for a boy.
And I hate a woman who puts out because she has to
    and stays dry, thinking about her wool.
Pleasure [*uoluptas*] that's given out of duty doesn't please me:
    let no girl do her duty for me.
I like to hear her words confess her raptures;
    I like to hear her ask me to slow down and keep it up.
Let me see my mistress out of her senses with passion, her eyes subdued;
    let her lie languid and forbid herself to be touched for a while.

Whatever Augustus thought of passages like these, it is clear that the Roman reading public ate them up. The elder Seneca (c. 50 BCE–c. 40 CE), an older contemporary of our poet, confirms Ovid's celebrity and quotes a description of him as "the poet who has filled this age not only with amatory *Arts* [a reference to the *Art of Love*] but also with amatory epigrams" (*Contr.* 3.7).

Ovid capped his three books on the *Art of Love* with a little book of *Cures for Love*, but he was far from finished with erotic themes. Although he transposed the carnal sexuality on display in his *Amores* and *Ars* to the plane of myth in the *Metamorphoses*, there is no diminution in the eroticism of his storytelling there. Indeed, many critics have seen love as a central theme of this, his only epic poem. At the end of the first century CE, for example, Quintilian noted the racy appeal of the *Metamorphoses* (*Inst. Or.* 10.1.88): "Ovid is certainly risqué [*lasciuus*] in his epic verses also, and too fond of his own wit, but nevertheless to be praised in parts." No doubt the *Metamorphoses* owes its enduring popularity in no small part to Ovid's lascivious verse, despite Quintilian's censure.[14] The myths selected for inclusion in this volume, for example, have often proved popular with Ovid's readers.

One of the most striking features of the sexual stories in the *Metamorphoses* is the sheer number of rape narratives in the poem—from Daphne to Philomela, Io and Callisto to Ganymede. Ovid himself comments on this feature of his poem in one of the most celebrated passages in the *Metamorphoses*, Arachne's tapestry (6.103–128), included as the first selection from the poem in the present volume. In artistic competition with Minerva, Arachne weaves a series of divine assaults on women, and there is a telling overlap in the thematic focus of her tapestry and that of the *Metamorphoses*. Thus, she begins with Jupiter's rape of Europa, which Ovid narrates at the end of *Metamorphoses* 2, and she continues with another eight of Jupiter's "amours," followed by six of Neptune, four of Apollo, and one each of Bacchus and Saturn: Asterie, Leda, Antiope, Alcmena, Danaë (4.611, 698) Aegina, Mnemosyne, Proserpina (5.515ff.); Canace, Theophane, Demeter, Medusa (4.785, 798ff.); Admetus, Melantho, Issa, and an unknown myth; Erigone (10.451) and Philyra (2.676). Ovid had already invoked, as the very "stuff" of his poetry, the rapes of Europa and Leda (and Io, whose myth he narrates at length in *Metamorphoses* 1) at the outset of his *Amores*, when promising his mistress immortality in verse (*Am.* 1.3.21–4, included in this volume). And although Ovid carefully avoids the repetition on Arachne's tapestry of the specific myths that he narrates elsewhere in the *Metamorphoses*, these very gods repeatedly ravish unsuspecting maidens and youths throughout the poem.

The gods surprise their victims often, though not exclusively, in the lush and verdant landscapes that Ovid describes so memorably in the *Metamorphoses*. I have argued elsewhere that classical poets repeatedly feminize and sexualize the landscapes in which they situate male action, and Ovid participates in this tradition in the *Metamorphoses*.[15] In the first book of the poem, for example, the floodwaters Jupiter sends to destroy the human race (sparing only Deucalion and Pyrrha) fertilize the earth, which regenerates the animal kingdom (1.416–437). Ovid represents Mother Earth metaphorically engaged in the process of child-bearing (1.416–417, 434–435), and he explicitly likens this metaphorical reproduction to the gestation of the child in the mother's womb (1.420). The generative female body is also a sexual body, however, so Ovid extends the metaphor that describes the earth as a reproductive body through the application of erotic vocabulary to describe the landscape as a sensual body. Ovid fleshes out the metaphor of the erotic landscape in a succession of erotic narratives in the *Metamorphoses*, including the salacious tale of the oversexed water nymph Salmacis and her spring's insalubrious effect on bathers in *Metamorphoses* 4. Introduced as a feature of the natural landscape, Salmacis is a clear Lycian spring (*lympha*), home to an indigenous nymph (*nympha*) of the same name. Ovid exploits a figural parallel between nymph and pool to describe Salmacis throughout the episode in diction applicable to both a woman and body of water (4.302–304, 309–316):

A nymph lived there, but not one who hunted
or bent a bow or ran hot in the races—

. . .

the only nymph quick Diana did not know.

. . .

She just bathed her lovely self in her pond,   310
often drew a boxwood comb through her hair,
or gazed in her glassy pool to see what looked best.
Sometimes, a see-through dress like light on her skin,
she lay back on the soft silky grass, the soft leaves;
often she picked flowers. She was picking flowers   315
when she saw the boy and wanted what she saw.

The interplay between spring and nymph is particularly well developed in the overlap between the attributes lacking to both. Just as the spring Salmacis lacks the Ovidian pool's customary accessories of reeds, sedge, and rushes with sharp points, so the nymph Salmacis foregoes the nymphs' customary activities of hunting and foot racing. Since rushes with sharp points characteristically supply the material for hunter's arrows with their own sharp points in the poem, their omission from the landscape in which the spring is set coheres with the nymph's lack of hunting paraphernalia. Moreover, Salmacis' lack of a hunting bow may be related to her spring's lack of a natural arch (the Latin word *arcus* is in the same in both cases), such as defines the setting in which Diana bathes earlier in the poem, when Actaeon unexpectedly spies her. The nymph's transparent clothing reflects the lucidity of her waters, and Salmacis' use of the clear waters of her spring as a mirror in which to check her appearance is paralleled by the description of her eyes blazing like the reflected image of the sun, as though her person exhibited the katoptric properties of a mirror.

Salmacis devotes herself to the pleasures of the flesh, rejecting the chaste pursuits of the goddess Diana in favor of the kind of sensual delights on display in Ovid's *Amores*, such as bathing, hair dressing, admiring her reflection, wearing transparent clothing, and lolling about on soft cushions. The final detail of Salmacis' pleasure in plucking flowers, however, ultimately differentiates her from the "over-painted nymphs" of Ovid's contemporary Rome, for it draws on the conventional epic association of the well-watered meadow with the rape of nymphs and other nubile maidens in classical literature (e.g., Proserpina in *Met.* 5). The epic topography of rape sets a maiden on the verge of marriage in a flowering landscape that figures her erotic appeal in the fountain ringed with grassy banks— in just such terms, indeed, as Salmacis and her spring are described (4.299–301): "and there he saw a still, deep pool, / translucent all the way down. Beside it grew / no marshy reeds, spiky rush, or swamp grass." The nubile maiden discovered in a *locus amoenus* landscape is conventionally plucked, like the metaphorical flower she is, by a divine rapist (i.e., she is deflowered). Earlier in the *Metamorphoses*, for example, Jupiter ravishes Io (1.588–600) and Callisto (2.409–431) in similar settings, while in the next book Dis will rape Proserpina as she picks flowers in a meadow beside Lake Henna in Sicily (5.385–395). But Salmacis will prove unexpectedly active, plucking the youth she admires rather than waiting for him to pluck her.

This survey of sexuality and gender has, inevitably, failed to do justice to the richness and complexity of these themes in Ovidian poetry. But Jane Alison's stylish renderings of Ovid's carnal verses in this volume beautifully capture their sensual appeal. Her assignment of passages from the *Metamorphoses* to thematic categories, moreover, invites our recognition of the Roman poet's kaleidoscopic play with sexual positions and gender norms, as displayed in the tale of Hermaphroditus and Salmacis, where a nymph overturns not only sexual codes and gender hierarchies, but also narrative conventions in her rape of a youth. The many myths of homoeroticism and trans-sexuality in Ovid's poetry, such as those of Hyacinth and of Iphis and Ianthe (both included in this volume), and his myths of incest such as those of Byblis, Myrrha, and Hippolytus (all included here), likewise exemplify Ovid's interest in transgressive sexuality and narrative ingenuity. The sexual postures of ruining someone, of looking and taking, of wanting someone too close, and changing direction all illuminate the facets of sexual and narrative desire with which Ovid experiments in his erotic verse, and which Jane Alison conveys so remarkably in her elegant translations.

Works Cited

Alison, J. 2001. *The Love-Artist*. New York.

Dover, J. K. 1978. *Greek Homosexuality*. London.

Foucault, M. 1976. *La Volenté de savoir*. Paris. Trans. R. Hurley, *The History of Sexuality, vol. 1: An Introduction*. New York 1980.

Gardner, H. 2013. *Gendering Time in Augustan Love Elegy*. Oxford.

James, S. 2003. *Learned Girls and Male Persuasion*. Berkeley.

Keith, A. M. 2000. *Engendering Rome: Women in Latin Epic*. Cambridge.

Keith, A. and Rupp, S. Eds. 2007. *Metamorphosis: The Changing Face of Ovid in Medieval and Early Modern Europe*. Toronto.

Martindale, C. 1988. *Ovid Renewed: Ovidian Influences on Literature and Art from the Middle Ages to the Twentieth Century*. Cambridge.

McGinn, T. A. J. 1998. *Prostitution, Sexuality, and the Law in Ancient Rome*. Oxford.

———. 2004. *The Economy of Prostitution in the Roman World: A Study of Social History and the Brothel*. Ann Arbor.

Sedgwick, E. K. 1992. *Between Men: English Literature and Male Homosocial Desire*. New York.
Skinner, M. B. 2005. *Sexuality in Greek and Roman Culture*. Malden MA and Oxford.
———. Ed. 2011. *A Companion to Catullus*. Malden MA and Oxford.
Stehle, E. 1997. *Performance and Gender in Ancient Greece*. Princeton.
Treggiari, S. 1991. *Roman Marriage: Iusti Coniuges from the Time of Cicero to the Time of Ulpian*. Oxford.
Williams, C. A. 1999. *Roman Homosexuality*. Oxford and New York. 2nd ed. 2010.
Wiseman, T. P. 1985. *Catullus and His World*. Cambridge.
Wray, D. 2001. *Catullus and the Poetics of Roman Manhood*. Cambridge.

Notes

1. The bibliography on sexuality and gender in classical antiquity is enormous. A good place to start is Skinner 2005.

2. On Greek homosexuality, see Dover 1978. On the legal, medical, and philosophical history of sexuality in classical antiquity, see also Foucault 1976 (English translation 1980).

3. On the temporal limits of a woman's sex appeal, see Gardner 2013.

4. Sappho is an obvious exception: on Sapphic sexuality, see Stehle 1997, 262–318.

5. Dover (1978) makes the argument, which has been widely accepted, at 100–9.

6. See Williams 1999.

7. Translations are my own and are literal rather than literary, intended to illustrate the larger discussion.

8. On Catullus' "homosocial" poetics of performative masculinity, see Wray 2001, 64–160. On "homosociality," see Sedgwick 1992.

9. On the scholarly debate, see Dyson Hejduk, Lorenc, and Gaisser in Skinner 2011.

10. On Catullus' social and literary circle, see Wiseman 1985.

11. I am indebted to the 1966 commentary of W. A. Camps in my translation of Prop. 2.7.

12. On the legislation, see Treggiari 1991 and McGinn 1998.

13. On the economic pressures on sex-workers in classical antiquity, see James 2003 and McGinn 2004. Jane Alison graphically depicts the violence of ancient abortion in her novel The Love-Artist, though she does not include Amores 2.13 and 14 in her selection of translations here.

14. In contrast to the hostile reception which Ovid's sexy poetry garnered among the political and scholastic authorities (like Augustus and Quintilian in antiquity), we may document its popularity among the reading public and, especially, among artists (literary, visual, musical) from antiquity to the present day. See Keith and Rupp 2007 and Martindale 1988.

15. Keith 2000.

FROM *AMORES*

• I.3

It's only fair: the girl who snared me should *love* me, too,
    or keep me in love forever.
Oh, I want too much: if she'll just endure my love,
    Venus will have granted my prayers.
5   Please take me. I'd be your slave year after long year.
    Please take me. I know how to love *true*.
I might not be graced with a grand family name,
    only knight-blood runs in my veins,
my acres might not need ploughs ad infinitum,
10   my parents count pennies, are tight—
but I've got Apollo, the Muses, and Bacchus,
    and Amor, who sent me your way,
plus true fidelity, unimpeachable habits,
    barest candor, blushingest shame.
15   I don't chase lots of girls—I'm no bounder in love.
    Trust me: you'll be mine forever.
I want to live with you each year the Fates spin me
    and die with you there to mourn.
Give me yourself—a subject perfect for poems—
20   they'll spring up, adorning their source.
Poems made Io (horrified heifer-girl) famous,
    plus that girl led on by a "swan"
and the one who set sail on a make-believe bull,
    his lilting horn tight in her fist.
25   We too will be famous, sung all over the world:
    my name bound forever to yours.

• I.4

So your man will be at the dinner party, too:
    I wish it were his last supper.
I'll only gaze at my darling, as any guest
    can? And *he'll* happily feel you
5   as you snuggle up properly there in his lap
    and stroke your neck if he likes?
Don't be surprised that fine Hippodameïa made
    those quasi-men brawl when drunk.

I don't live in the woods or trot around half a horse
    yet still can't keep my hands off you.   10
Now pay attention to what you must do and don't let
    my words flutter off in the winds.
Get there before he does. What we can do if you do
    I don't know, but still, get there first.
When he pats the couch, look modest and settle beside   15
    him—but flick my foot as you pass.
Watch me when I talk, note my nods and expressions;
    catch my subtle signs and respond.
I'll utter meaningful words not by voice but by brow,
    words written by finger in wine.   20
Whenever you ponder our last playtime in bed
    touch a thumb to your pinkening cheek;
if there's something you're longing to scold me about
    let your hand float by your ear;
but when I say or do anything, Sunshine, you like   25
    keep turning and turning your ring.
Put your hands on the table as you do when you pray
    if you're wishing your man the worst.
If he mixes your wine, be smart: make *him* drink it;
    tell the boy yourself what you want.   30
When you hand back your cup I'll snatch it up first—
    where your lips sipped, mine will sip, too.
But if he offers a nibble of something he's tried,
    refuse tidbits touched by his mouth.
Do *not* rest your neck on that arm draped around you,   35
    don't lean your head on his bony chest
or his fingers might slip through a sleeve to a touchable breast . . .
    Absolutely do not kiss him.
If you kiss him just once, I'll declare I'm your lover,
    cry 'Those kisses are mine!' and take them.   40
But all of this I can see. It's what coverlets hide
    that's got me scared nearly blind.
Don't snuggle your thigh with his, do *not* nudge his calf
    or twine your soft foot with his—hoof.
God, I'm afraid: I've done so much outrageous myself   45
    I'm racked by my own example.
Often my lover and I, under cover, have hurried
    each other to that sweet melting end.

You'll never do that. But so you won't look like you did . . .
50   be sure those regions aren't cloaked.
Urge fresh drinks on your man (no need to add kisses);
         as he swallows, slip in more wine.
If he's resting in peace, soundly sodden and snoring,
         what we can do, where—we'll find fast.
55   When everyone stands up to go home, and you, too,
         move straight to the knot in the crowd:

you'll find me there in the throng, or else I'll find you—
         and if you can touch me, please *do*.
But oh god, all this will help just a handful of hours:
60   I'm kept from you by order of night.
That's when he jails you. So, spilling tears, I'll do all I can:
         slump outside your door, despondent.
While inside he'll kiss you—and not only kiss you.
         What you sneak me, pay him as tax.
65   Yes: do it only unwilling (you can), under force;
         whisper sweet *nothing*. (Venus: be cold!)
And if my wish can come true, I wish him no pleasure:
         positively no pleasure for you.
But whatever does happen to happen tonight,
70   tomorrow, deny anything did.

·   I.5

◄))   Scorching hot, and the day had drifted past noon;
         I spread out on my bed to rest.
Some slats of the windows were open, some shut,
         the light as if in a forest
5   or like the sinking sun's cool glow at dusk
         or when night wanes, but dawn's not come.
It was the sort of light that nervous girls love,
         their shyness hoping for shadows.
And oh—in slips Corinna, her thin dress unsashed,
10   hair rivering down her pale neck,
just as lovely Sameramis would steal into a bedroom,
         they say, or Lais, so loved by men.
I pulled at her dress, so scant its loss barely showed,
         but still she struggled to keep it.

Though she struggled a bit, she did not want to win: 15
    undone by herself, she gave in.
When she stood before me, her dress on the floor,
    her body did not have a flaw.
Such shoulders I saw and touched—oh, such arms.
    The form of her breast firm in my palm,   20
and below that firm fullness a belly so smooth—
    her long shapely sides, her young thighs!
Why list one by one? I saw nothing not splendid
    and clasped her close to me, bare.
Who can't guess the rest? And then we lay languid.   25
    Oh, for more middays just so.

•   2.12

Laurels of triumph on my head, please: I've won!
    Corinna is here in my lap,
though her hateful husband, guard, and locked doors kept watch
    in case she be charmed away.
And this conquest of mine deserves a full-scale parade   5
    because the plunder was bloodless.
No little mud walls, no townlets ringed by minor moats:
    my generalship got *me* a girl.
When Troy finally fell after ten years of war,
    all those men—how much done by the chief?   10
But *my* glory's my own, no other soldiers involved,
    no one else gets my badge of service.
I got what I wanted as general and army; I was
    horseman, soldier—and carried the flag.
Chance played no part in how my battles were won: 15
    hail, conquest by pure attention!
Why my war? Nothing new. If Helen hadn't been snatched,
    Asia'd be allied with Europe.
A *woman* turned woodsy Lapiths on the half-and-half
    herd, sickeningly slopped with wine.   20
A *woman* made Trojans fight all over again,
    this time with your kingdom, Latinus.
A *woman*—when the city of Rome was still new—
    stirred her in-laws to fierce attack.

25   I've seen bulls stamp and gore for a milky young bride;
        gazing on, she only provoked them.
    Cupid's called many to carry his flag, and me, too—
        but I do it shedding no blood.

  ◆   **3.4**

Oh you tough man, guarding that girl gets you nothing:
    her proclivities are what count.
If she's faithful without threats, she's really faithful;
    but if with no choice, she's not.
5   Lock up her body—but an adulterous mind can't be
    controlled: it'll crave all it can get.
No, you can't guard her body even locking the doors:
    all men are outside—the cheat's in.
Someone allowed to stray never strays far: sheer license
10   makes those wicked seeds sluggish.
Trust me and stop: your rules only arouse her lust;
    indulgence will undo her better.
I just saw a horse fighting the bit gripped in its mouth
    yet that bit made it bolt like lightning;
15   but the instant it felt the reins droop and the bridle drop
    slack on its mane—it stopped short.
We always chase what we can't have, itch for what's banned:
    the sick man prescribed *dry* wants *wet*.
A hundred eyes on Argus' face, on his neck a hundred
20   more, but Amor often duped him.
Danaë entered an impregnable stone bedroom a virgin—
    but still she came out a mother.
Yet Penelope stayed pure among lusty young suitors
    although there was no guard in sight.
25   What's protected we want even more; gates only entice
    a thief. Who lusts for what's easy?
It's not her looks that stir men but her husband's obsession—
    something has got to beguile him.
A girl on a leash doesn't grow good but a coveted cheat:
30   fear hikes the price of her body.
You might disapprove, but forbidden pleasure's more fun:
    she whispers, "I'm scared"—I'm excited.

But of course you can't lock up a woman who's freeborn;
    intimidation's for foreigners.
Plus if your watchdog can claim that *he's* done the job—   35
    your slave is praised for her purity?
A man's a big fool if his wife's philandering hurts,
    ill-informed of our city's past—
why, its foundlings, Mars' boys, were conceived in sin, too:
    Ilia's Romulus and Remus.   40
Why choose a beauty if it's devotion you wanted?
    The two don't come in one shape.
If you're smart, indulge your lady, stop looking so stern,
    don't lay down law like a strongman
and enjoy the new friends she gets you (she'll get you lots):   45
    favors will flow without effort!
You'll always be allowed to go drink with the boys,
    have a house full of gifts got for free.

• 3.11

I've stood so much for so long; now I'm through with your tricks.
    Sick love, leave my heart: it's done.
I've served my time but have broken free of these chains—
    wasn't sorry to bear them, *now* sorry I did.
But I've won and I'm crushing Love under my foot.   5
    I've finally sprouted a backbone.
Hold up. Be tough. One day this pain will pay off:
    a bitter drink can be bracing.
Did I really put up with rejection so often, setting my
    thoroughbred self in the dirt by your door?   10
Did I really sleep outside your dark house like a slave,
    while inside you loved up some no one?
I've seen a worn-out lover stumble from your front gate
    and stagger home, spent, service done.
Still, this is far better than him seeing *me*:   15
    I'd wish that shame on enemies.
But when did I ever not cleave close beside you,
    your protector, your man, your friend?
Of course being with *me* made you a popular darling:
    my love is what launched your affairs.   20

Oh why tell the sickening lies that slid from your tongue
    or oaths broken at my expense
or the meaningful nods of strange men at parties
    or messages coded in signs?
25   I'm told she's ill: I bolt to her house, rushing with love.
    I get there: she's not sick for *him*.
I've put up with this and more I won't say: now I'm tough.
    Find someone else to endure you.
My ship's floating becalmed with a garland of thanks,
30   aloof from the wild swelling sea.
So stop your sweet nothings. To hell with words so magical
    once. I'm not the fool I was.

(b)

My mercurial heart's a tempest, blowing opposite ways—
    now love, now hate. I think love'll win.
[[]]37(5)   I run from your worthlessness, am dragged back by your looks.
    I hate your corruption; your body, I love.
So I'm unable to live either with or without you
40   and don't seem to know what I want.
I wish you were either less bad or less lovely:
(10)   your looks don't deserve wicked ways.
What you do makes me hate you, your face cries for love:
    oh god, beauty undoes her badness.
45   Spare me, by the secrets we've whispered in bed,
    by the gods you so often cheat,
(15)   by your beauty, which seems almost holy to me . . .
    and your eyes, which have made me blind.
Whatever you'll be, you'll always be mine. Do you want me
50   to want you, or love you by force?
Let me unfurl sails, fly with following winds, and *want* what
(20)   I must love, even if I don't want.

• 3.12

What day was it, blackbirds, that you cawed your bleak
    Nevermore to me, ever in love?
Should I wonder what stars have crisscrossed my fate
    or ask which gods war against me?

The girl who's supposed to be mine to love, mine *alone*,   5
    I dread is now open to all.
Am I wrong, or did my own books make her famous?
    Yes: she's on sale thanks to my talent.
I deserve it. What made me broadcast her beauty?
    My fault the girl's on the market.   10
I've pimped her delights; torched the way for a lover;
    my hands have flung open her door.
If they do good I don't know; poems surely do bad:
    my successes stirred up envy.
It could have been Thebes or Troy or Caesar's achievements—   15
    only Corinna inspired me.
I wish the Muses had stoppered their ears to my poems
    and Apollo had dimmed at my drafts.
But poets aren't usually considered so *credible* . . .
    I didn't mean to seem so *concrete*.   20
What we poets do: make Scylla snip her father's rare lock
    then grow dogs from her loins and hips;
we sprout feathers from feet, and serpents from hair,
    and have Perseus ride a winged horse.
We stretch giant Tityos across acres of land and   25
    triple-head a dog with a snake-tail;
we make Enceladon a thousand arms for his spears,
    ensnare men with mergirls who sing.
We envelop winds in a skin-bag for Ulysses,
    let traitor Tantalus thirst in a stream;   30
we turn Niobe to granite, Callisto to bear, and let
    Philomela hush Itys as swallow.
We have Jupiter melt down to gold or be bird
    or cleave seas as bull, maiden-mounted.
Why mention Proteus or Theban teeth that were seeds,   35
    those bulls that snorted out fire,
the sisters of Phaethon who wept amber tears,
    the boats transformed to sea-nymphs,
the sun that set fast when Atreus roasted a nephew,
    or stones rolling in time to a lute?   40
Poetic invention blooms to the fathomless blue,
    its words free from historical "truth."
The girl I sang to the skies should have seemed made-up, too!
    Your gullibility—is my ruin.

FROM *METAMORPHOSES*

I. *Looking*

- I . 1

ARACHNE (6.1–145)

When Minerva heard the story the Muses sang
she approved both their song and their anger
and said, "Praise isn't enough. I *should* be praised,
and anyone shunning me should be punished."
5   She pondered Arachne, a girl from Maeonia
who (she'd heard) would not admit that *she* wove
best. In homeland and bloodline the girl wasn't much:
but art made her shine. Her father, Idmon of Colophon,
dipped in sea-snail purple her thirsty wool;
10   her mother was dead but lower class, too, the same
as her husband. Still, the girl had won a name
for skill all over the Lydian towns, even if
she lived in a hovel in little Hypaepa.
To have a look at the wonders she wove
15   the nymphs of Tmolus kept leaving their thickets,
the nymphs of Pactolus kept leaving their streams.
Not only the cloths she'd woven: they loved to watch
her weave them, too. There was such grace in her art!
Whether she wound the raw wool into balls,
20   or kneaded the stuff with fingertips, then drew
it out and drew again to make strands light as cloud
or spun the polished spindle quick with a thumb or
needlepointed pictures: Minerva'd surely shown her.

But she said no, insulted by even this teacher.
25   "Let's compete," she said. "I'll stake all I have if I lose."
Minerva turned herself old, frosting her hair
and using a cane to help her wobbling, weak legs.

Then she said, "Not everything about old age
is repulsive; there's value in living long years.
Take my advice: seek all the fame you can win   30
in the human sphere for what you do with wool,
but give in to a goddess—in fact, beg her pardon
for your outrageous words: she'll give it if you ask."
The girl glowered at Minerva (in disguise) and put
down the strands she'd begun. She held back her hands   35
but her face showed her fury. "Here you've come,"
she said, "feeble-minded and drained by old age—
you've lived too long: that's your trouble. Waste your words
on your daughter or son's wife, if you have them.
My advice suits me fine. And so you won't think   40
your warning's moved me, my opinion's as it was.
Why doesn't she come, then? Why won't she compete?"
"I've come!" said the goddess, shed the old-woman guise,
and stood there, Minerva herself. The nymphs and women
of Mygdonia bowed: only the girl wasn't scared.   45
But she flushed: a sudden blush filled her face—
she couldn't control it—but vanished as fast,
just as the sky grows plum when dawn first comes
but with sunrise, soon glows white.
She persists in what she's done, lusting for a silly   50
prize, rushing to her ruin. For Jove's child won't say
no to her now, warn again, or put off the contest.

No time to waste: the two set up in separate
stations and stretch fine threads upon twinned looms.
Each binds warp to beam, combs yarn with a reed,   55
threads the weft in and out with a shuttle that's led
by her fingertips, and once it's laced through the web,
the notched teeth of the reed tap it neatly in place.
Both work quickly, dresses ribboned to chests
as skillful hands glide, their effort glossed by zeal.   60
Woven in is purple concocted in Tyrian pots
and delicate shades that invisibly shift
as when sunrays shine through a shower of rain
and a rainbow curves color across the wide sky;
in it glows the whole spectrum of hues,   65
but from one to the next a haze fools our eyes.

Each shade like the next, but the ends: so distant!
Woven in too is wiry gold thread—
and plotted into each web are old stories.

70   Minerva portrays the Hill of Mars in Athens
and the ancient quarrel over naming the place.
The heavenly gods are throned around Jove,
all with august gravity. To each god she gives
the proper features: Jove's the image of King.
75   The god of the sea she has standing and striking
the crag with his trident, and from the split stone
springs salty sea, and this is his claim to the city.
To herself she gives shield and sharp-pointed spear,
helmet on head, aegis hiding her breast.
80   She shows herself jabbing the earth with her spear
and up springs a sapling olive, silver with fruit,
as the gods marvel, and Victory crowns her work.

So this praise-hungry girl will understand
the real prize she'll get for her outrageous claim,
85   Minerva shows a contest in each of four corners,
each with bright colors and its own little forms.
In one corner: Thracian Rhodope and Haemus,
cold craggy mountains, though they'd been human
until they stole the lofty gods' names for themselves.
90   The next corner portrays the poor Pygmy queen
and her fate: once Juno had beaten her in a game,
she made her a crane and turned her on her former folk.
Next she wove Antigone, who once dared compete
with the wife of great Jove, so Juno transformed
95   her into a bird, and neither Troy nor her father
Laomedon could help—clad in white feathers
she's now a stork, clattering and clapping her beak.
The last corner shows Cinyras, stripped of children,
as he clutches the steps of a temple that had
100   once been his daughters and lies weeping on the stone.
She rims the whole cloth with her peaceful olive,
making her own tree the finale: *The End.*

Arachne weaves Europa tricked by a make-believe
bull: but you'd think it's a *real* bull and a real sea.

You can see the girl gaze at the shore left behind   105
and cry to her friends as she shivers to touch
the jostling waves, holding up her nervous feet.
She shows Asterie clasped by the straining eagle
and Leda lounging in the wings of a swan;
she shows how Jove masqueraded as satyr   110
to fill lovely Antiope with twins, but snared
Alcmena as if her husband, and Danaë as if
he were gold; he came as flame to Aegina,
shepherd to Mnemosyne; Proserpina—snake.
And she stitched you, Neptune, also: as a bull   115
you raged for Canace; as Enipeus you sired
the Aloides; you tricked Theophane as ram;
the gentle flaxen mother of wheat felt you as
a horse; the snake-haired mother of the winged horse
felt something likewise winged; Melantho felt a dolphin.   120
To each she gave the proper face and appearance
of the place. Here's Apollo looking rustic;
here he has a falcon's wings; there, a lion's pelt;
he tricks Macareus' child Issa as shepherd;
Bacchus dupes Erigone with artificial grapes;   125
Saturn sires the centaur Chiron as a horse.
And she edges the web with a narrow trim
of flowers, interwoven with ivy entwined.

Neither Minerva nor gnawing Envy could niggle
with the work. Her triumph pained the golden goddess: 130
she ripped that cloth colored with godly assaults
and, clutching her shuttle of Cytorian boxwood,
hit Arachne three or four times in the head.
The girl couldn't bear it and slipped a noose around
her pounding throat. But Minerva pitied and lifted   135
her, saying, "Live on, bold girl, but hang all the same.
So you'll be worried for the future as well,
may your line bear this punishment always."

As she left, she threw juice of Hecate's herb
on the girl. At once the poisonous potion   140
made her hair fall away, her nose and ears, too.
Her head became small—her body went tiny:
her fingers crept as little legs to her sides;

the rest of her was stomach. From it still she spins
145   out silk, weaving her old webs, now a spider.

·   I . 2

DAPHNE   (1.452–567)

Apollo's first love was Daphne, child of river god
Peneus—and not by chance, but Cupid's cruel rage.
Apollo (still proud of his fresh kill: the Python)
455   saw Cupid bend his bow, pulling the cord, and said
"What's a playboy like you got to do with big weapons?
Those massive things belong on *my* shoulders—
I who render lethal blows to enemies and beasts,
I who just laid out over acres that bloated snake,
460   its poison-fat belly riddled by a million darts.
You, be happy singeing people, making them fall
in love, or whatever: don't try stealing my glory."
Cupid said, "Your arrows hit everything, but mine
will hit you, and as far below gods as animals
465   are, that's how far your glory is below mine."
Then he blasted the air with wings beating hard
and stopped sharp at the shady peak of Parnassus.
He pulled two shafts from his quiver of arrows, shafts
with different points: one prevents love, one injects it.
470   (The first arrow's gold, with a fine, gleaming tip;
the other is dull, its shaft thickened with lead.)
With the dull one he pierced Peneus' child—then shot
the sharp one through Apollo's bone, to his marrow.

◀ঃ   At once one's in love; the other runs from the word
475   and delights in the shadowy woods and the hides
of creatures she's captured, like virgin Diana.
[]478   Many men want her, but she says no—she wants
nothing of men and roams untrodden woods, with no
480   interest in Hymen, love, or matters like marriage.
Her father would say, "You owe me a son-in-law, girl."

Or he'd say, "Child, you owe me some grandchildren."
As horrified by marriage as by some crime,
she'd blush, embarrassed, her pretty face bright,
throw winning arms around his neck and cry,   485
"Dear adorable father, please let me stay
a virgin girl always. Diana's father lets *her*."
So he did. But, Daphne, your beauty won't let you
stay as you like: your looks sabotage your longings.

Apollo loves, wants to wed this Daphne he sees.   490
What he wants he expects: his foretelling fails him.
As the frizzled beards of reaped corn will burn
or a hedge will catch fire if a traveler veers too
close with his torch or leaves it behind at daybreak,
so the god bursts into flame, passion flaring   495
in his heart: he feeds hopeless love by hoping.
Gazing at hair fallen loose on her neck, he says
"What if she did it up?" He stares ablaze at eyes
like sparkling stars; looks at her mouth, and just looking
won't do; praises her fingers and hands and wrists   500
and arms that are bare almost all the way up;
what's hidden he's sure is better. But she flits off
quick and light as wind, won't stop to hear him calling
"Nymph, please, Peneia, wait! I'm not hunting you—
wait! A lamb bolts from a wolf, deer from a lion,   505
and doves flutter fearful away from an eagle,
each from its enemy. But I'm chasing for *love*.
Oh no—please don't stumble and fall, let brambles
scratch your blameless legs, with me the cause of pain!
The places you're running are rough. Run more slowly,   510
please, don't flee so fast; I'll chase more slowly, too.
Or ask who it is that likes you so: no mountain boy
or shepherd—not me. I'm no hairy brute watching
cows or sheep. You don't know, flighty girl, you don't know
who you flee—that's *why* you flee. I'm lord of Delphi!   515
And Claros, Tenedos, and Patara are mine.
My father's Jove! Through me, what will be, was, and *is*
grow clear; it's me who gives songs their music.
My arrows are sure but an arrow still surer
has made out of nothing this pain in my heart.   520

I first made medicine—I'm called *The Healer*
all over the world—it's from me herbs have strength.
But, oh me, no herb can cure love, and my skills
that do such good in the world do me no good at all."

525   For Daphne had fled on her panicked path, leaving
him saying all this and about to say more,
but this suited her, too. The wind bared her body,
breeze flowing through her fluttering dress,
light air streaming the hair out behind her—

530   more lovely even leaving. The young god cannot
waste more time with sweet words so, taking advice
from Amor himself, runs after her full speed.
As when a greyhound spots a hare in a field
and he gallops for her, she for her life,

535   and the one is certain now, certain to seize
her, and grazes her foot with straining jaws,
and she, not sure if she's already caught, rips
clear from those fangs just as they touch her, away—
so run god and girl, he sped by hope, she by fear.

540   But the one spurred by Love is faster and will not
let her catch her breath, touches her back as she flees,
and breathes on the hair flying loose at her neck.

543   Her energy wanes and she goes pale, undone,

544a   and when she sees the Peneus glint, she cries,
"Help me, Father, if there's mystic strength in your stream,

547   destroy this form that's too pleasing: change me."
Words barely uttered when slowness seeps in her limbs,
delicate bark nestles around her soft breasts,

550   her hair fans into leaves, arms lengthen to branches,
the feet just so quick sink down sluggish as roots,
her face turns leafy crown: all that stays is splendor.
Apollo loves her this way, too, touches the trunk,
can feel the nymph's heart beating beneath the new bark.

555   Holding a branch like an arm in his own, he kisses
the wood, but even it shrinks away from that kiss.
So the god says, "Since you cannot be my bride,
you will be my tree, laurel, and your leaves
will twine about my hair, quiver, and lute.

560   You'll be with Roman leaders when the song of glory's

sung and the Capitol sees parades of triumph;
you'll stand as faithful sentinel by the twin gates
of Augustus and guard the oak wreath hung between.
And as my head is young, my hair's never shorn,
you too will have forever an evergreen grace."   565
The Healer was done. The laurel made a sign
with her branches, seemed to shake her leafy crown.

· I . 3

ACTAEON   (3.138–252)

Amid such happy times, Cadmus, your grandson   🔊
was first to cause you pain—strange antlers sprouting
from his brow, those dogs that drank their master's blood.   140
If you look closely, you'll blame the boy's Fortune,
not a crime. How can a mistake be a crime?

The hills were stained with blood of animals killed,
midday had pulled shadows close to their owners,
and the sun hung midway between east and west   145
when young Actaeon, with his gentle face, called
his fellow hunters as they tramped the wilds:
"Our nets and knives drip with animal blood, boys—
we've had enough fortune for now. When a new dawn
rolls in on saffron wheels and brings a fresh day,   150
we'll resume what we've begun. But now Apollo's
burning at his height and cracks the fields with heat,
so set down your work; take up the tangled nets."
The men did, putting aside their tasks for the day.

There's a valley dense with needled cypress and pine   155
called Gargaphie, dear to high-skirted Diana.
In its deepest hollow is a mossy cavern
carved not by art, but nature has conjured art
in her ingenious way: from airy pumice
and delicate tufa she's shaped a natural arch.   160

Bright lines of water plash from a spring at one side
and flow into a pool encircled with grass.
The goddess of woodlands, exhausted from stalking,
likes to bathe her pure limbs in this water and mist.
165   She's come here today and gives her unstrung bow,
quiver and spear to one of her nymphs to hold
as one drapes on an arm the robe she's slipped off
and two untie her boots. Pebble from Thebes is more
skillful than they and loops hair loose at Diana's
170   neck in a knot, though her own hair tumbles undone.
Then Purity, Glass, Raindrop, Sparkle, and Dish
scoop up water in deep urns, and pour it.

As Diana bathed here in her favorite pool,
look—Cadmus' grandson, his work put aside, came
175   wandering these strange woods with faltering steps,
wandering into the grove, led by his dark fate.
As soon as he entered the cave misty with spray
and the nymphs spotted a man, they struck their breasts,
bare as they were, flooded the grove with startled
180   cries, and ran to ring Diana, trying to hide
her body with theirs. But the goddess was more tall
than her nymphs and rose shoulders and head above them.
The color of clouds stained by the sun as it sinks
or the rosy blush you see at dawn: this flush filled
185   Diana's face as she stood still, naked and seen.
Although her flock of followers clung to her close,
she held her face and body turned to the side;
and though she wished she had arrows to hand,
she scooped up water, flung it at the man's face,
190   scattered vengeful drops on his hair, and added
words to seal the disaster soon coming:
"Now you can tell everyone you've seen me undressed—
that is, if you can tell anything." Warning no more,
she sprouted live antlers from the head she'd just wet
195   and pulled his neck long and his ears to fine tips;
she turned his arms and hands to skinny shanks
and hooves, and coated his body in dappled hide;
she also threw in fear. And away flit the hero,
Autonoë's son, startled by his sudden new speed.

He would have cried "Oh me," but no voice came.   []201
He moaned, that voice came, but no tears could flow
from his eyes: yet inside his old thoughts remained.
What could he do? Go home to his palace or hide
in the woods? Shame blocked one move, fear the other.   205

As he wavers, the hunting dogs spot him. Blackfoot
and sly Tracker break the news with their barks:
Blackfoot's from Sparta, Tracker's from Crete.
Then the others come galloping faster than wind,
Guzzler and Brighteye and Ranger—Arcadian—   210
and brave Bamboozle, harsh Cyclone, and Beast;
Wing (of quick foot) and Trap (of quick nose)
and Woody, just tusked by a savage wild boar,
and Gully, who's half wolf; Heidi, who herds
sheep, and Greedy's along too with her pups;   215
and Sicyonian Snatch with the scrawny flanks
and Runner and Clash and Spot, Tiger, and Tough,
and Whitey with pale fur and Sooty with dark
and spectacular Spartan and fast-footed Eddy
and Speedy and Wolf with quick brother Cyprius   220
and Stealer whose black head is spotted with white,
and Blacky and that furry one, Fluff—
both suckled by Sparta but sired by Crete—
and Fury, Whitefang, and high-barking Howler
and—too long to name the rest. The bloodthirsty pack   225
chases its prey over crags, cliffs, impossible
boulders: rough going when there's going at all.
He runs through regions he's so often hunted
and oh! he flees his own friends. He wants to cry out—
no words in his mind: the sky rings instead with baying.   []231
Blackhair tears the first hole in his back,
Hunter is next, while Hiker fixes fangs in his arm
(they left home late, but a shortcut through gullies
let them catch up). As they pin down their master   235
the pack rushes in and sets teeth in his flesh.
Soon no place is left to rip; he groans a sound
that doesn't seem human but could be cried
by no stag and fills the hills he's known so well
with cries of grief, then on his knees he begs   240

not with pleading arms but with a silent face.
His friends goad the frenzied pack with the usual
shouts, and they look for Actaeon, with no idea,
and bellow for Actaeon, as if he weren't there
245 (at his name he lifts his head), and they're mad
the slacker's missed the show and will not see the prize.
He'd rather miss this but he's there; he'd rather
see than feel his own dogs' ravenous ripping.
They cluster upon him, muzzles deep in his flesh,
250 and tear apart master falsely figured as stag.
Not until all his many wounds wane away his life
is the fury of quivered Diana appeased.

· I . 4

ECHO AND NARCISSUS (3.339–510)

Tiresias was famous in the towns of Boeotia
340 for telling true futures to those wanting to know.
The first to see if his words came true was wet
blue Liriope, whom Cephisos had pulled
down in his twisting currents and taken
there by force. The lovely nymph had a child,
345 an alluring baby even then, and called the boy
Narcissus. When she asked the prophet if
her boy would live long and see many years
he said, "As long as he never knows himself."
For a time these words seemed empty, but at last
350 the boy's end and strange madness turned them true.

For when Narcissus had just turned sixteen
he looked as much a young man as a boy,
and many girls, many boys wanted him badly,
but (in his lean body was such cold pride)
355 that no girls, no boys could touch him.
Seeing him drive frightened deer into nets
was that chattery nymph who couldn't keep quiet

or start talking herself, poor clamoring Echo.
She still had a body, she wasn't just voice,
yet could use her mouth then only as she does now: 360
helplessly repeating the last words someone says.
Juno had done this: for each time she was set
to pounce upon nymphs rolling with Jove in the hills,
clever Echo caught her in long conversation
so the nymphs could scatter. When Juno saw, she said   365
"That tongue of yours that tricked me will be limp
and worthless now, and your voice will be—oh, useless."
Her threat came true at once: Echo singsongs back
another's voice and parrots the words she's heard.

When she saw Narcissus roam alone in the woods   370
she was excited at once and secretly trailed,
and the closer she followed the hotter she grew,
as when sulfur is daubed at the top
of a torch and snatches the dancing flames.
Oh, how she wanted to go with sweet words and say   375
how she longed for him! But her nature stopped this,
would let her start nothing. So she would wait
and do all she could: cry back any words he said.
The boy had somehow lost his close gang of friends
so called, "Is anyone here?" "Here!" called Echo.   380
He was surprised, looked around, and then shouted
"Come!"—and she shouted it back to him shouting.
He looked again, and when nobody came, he called
"Why stay away from me?"—she called the same.
He stood still, tricked by the sense of an answering voice, 385
and cried, "Be with me, come!" Never more lustily
would Echo cry any words: "Be with me, come!"
And she herself followed these words from the woods,
rushing to throw her arms around his sweet neck.
But he bolted and, bolting, shouted, "Hands off!   390
I would die before I'd give you anything."
Stricken, she could only say, "I'd give you anything . . ."
Then she hid in the woods, kept her mortified face
muffled in leaves, and lived only in lonely caves.
But her love clung, swelled with painful rejection;   395
sleeplessness wasted away her poor flesh

and pulled her gaunt and tight. Her freshness and sap
drifted into air; only voice and bones remained.
Then voice alone—they say her bones became rock.

[[]]402   So Narcissus teased her and other nymphs of streams
and steep hills, as well as mobs of young men.
Then one boy he'd refused raised his arms to the sky
405   and said, "Let him love, too, but not get what he loves."
Nemesis heard this fair prayer and said, *Yes.*
There was a clear pool with a glittering shine
that no shepherds or nibbling mountain goats
or flock had ever found, that no bird or wild
410   creature or crashing branch had ever troubled.
Grass growing around it drank from the pool,
and the sheltering trees let no sun warm the spot.
Worn out by hunting and heat, the boy is drawn
to the look of the place and its pool and sinks down;
[]416   as he drinks, he's entranced by the image he sees.
[]418   Amazed by himself, he holds his face rapt
and sits still, like a figure of Parian marble.
420   Lying prone, he gazes at twin stars, his eyes,
and hair that could belong to Apollo or Bacchus,
and peachfuzz cheeks, ivory neck, delectable
mouth, and snowflake paleness tinged by a blush—
he admires everything for which he's admired.
425   Knowing no better, he loves himself, praises, is praised,
wants and is wanted, both lights the match and burns.
How often he tries kissing that shimmering pool!
How often he plunges hands deep into water
to touch the neck he admires, but clasps only wet!
430   He doesn't know what he sees, but what he sees burns;
the delusion deceiving his eyes lures them deep.
Trickable boy, why try to catch a flittering image?
What you look for is nowhere: what you love—turn, it's gone.
What you see is a shadow, a glimmer reflected:
435   it's nothing alone. It comes with you, stays,
and will go with you, too—if indeed you can go.

No need for food or even sleep can pull the boy
away. He stretches out on the dusky grass

and can't keep his eyes from his own slippery form:
his eyes will be his end. He props himself up,   440
holds out arms to the trees all around, and says
"Woods, has anyone been more cruelly in love?
You've been the secret place for so many, you'd know.
The centuries you've been alive: do you recall
in your long years anyone as ruined as me?   445
I see what I want. But what I see, what I want,
I just cannot get." (The lover's in such a maze!)
"What makes it worse: between us is no sea,
no highway or mountains or walls with locked gates:
just a shine of water. He wants to be held—   450
each time my lips touch the bright liquid to kiss,
he bends to me, too, his face tilted, too.
You'd think I could touch him: so little blocks love.
Whoever you are, come! Why tease me, lone boy,
or slip off when I seek you? Surely my looks and age   455
can't repel you—even nymphs have adored me.
What hope your face offers I cannot quite read,
but when I reach for you, you reach for me, too;
when I smile, so do you; and I've spotted tears
on your face when I cry. You signal with nods   460
and I can guess by your sweet murmuring mouth
that you answer my words with *yours*—I can't hear.
I am he. I knew, my image doesn't delude me.
I burn with love for myself, fan and feel the same flames.
What do I do? Chase or be chased? Why chase at all?   465
What I want I have: needing nothing makes me poor.
Oh, if only my body and I could divide!
Odd wish for a lover: to want the loved one to go.
This hopelessness will kill me; I can't have long
to live and will be put out while still young.   470
But death doesn't disturb me—no more despair.
Only I wish the one I love could live longer.
Now the two of us will die with one breath."

He said this, broke down, turned back to that face,
and troubled the water with tears, the image   475
reflected in pieces. When it rippled apart
he cried, "Where are you going? Stay here, mean boy,

don't leave your lover. I may not touch you,
but at least I can look and feed my sick love."
480   As he wept he pulled the cloak from his shoulder
and beat his bare breast with marblewhite hands.
And where he had struck, the skin blushed pink,
like apples that are pale in some places,
ripe red in others, or like grapes in a motley
485   cluster that aren't yet ripe but tinged with mauve.
When he saw this, once the water had stilled,
he could take no more. But as yellow wax
softens in a gentle flame, or morning frost
becomes liquid in sun, so, wasted by love,
490   he slowly dissolved, melted by the fire within.
Now there's no more paleness blushed with pink,
no flush of vigor or life, no luring looks,
nothing left of the body Echo had loved.
But as she watched, though still hurt, her memory
495   aching, each time the poor boy cried, "Oh no,"
her voice echoed it into the air: *Oh no . . .*
When he struck his own shoulders in dismay,
she echoed the sad sounds of these strokes.
His last words, as he gazed into his pool:
500   "Oh, boy, loved for nothing." The place called his words
too, and to his "Goodbye" *Goodbye* echoed.
At last he lay his head on the green grass
and death closed the eyes entranced by their master.
(But even in the Underworld, he would gaze
505   in the waters of Styx.) His sister Naiads
wept, grieved, and cut their hair for their brother,
and the Dryads, too; Echo mirrored their weeping.
They prepared funeral pile, flaming torches, and bier—
but found no body. No body—but a blossom
510   of white petals around a burning yellow heart.

◆ I.5

PERSEUS AND ANDROMEDA (AND MEDUSA)   (4.614–803)

. . . one brother took a place in heaven while the other
clutched his haunting trophy, that horror of snakes,   615
and sheared through the air with his whistling wings.
When Perseus coasted over Libya's wastes,
drops of blood leaking from the Gorgon's head fell—
once each sank into sand it squirmed to life as a snake.
This land has teemed, since; it wriggles with vipers.   620

Then blustering winds drive him through fathomless
skies, wafting him here and there like a cloud.
From high in the air as he whirls over the world
he gazes down at lands set far from the sea.
Thrice he sees the icy Bears; thrice, the clawing Crab;   625
often he's swept to the west; often, to the east.
Now as daylight fades, afraid of flying at night,
he lands in western lands governed by Atlas
and hopes for some sleep until the Morning Star
wakes glowing Dawn, and Dawn, the wheeling daylight.   630
Here stands Atlas, son of Iapetus, his body more
giant than any man. He's the king of the ends
of the world and the sea whose waves water the Sun's
panting horses and welcome his hot, creaking car.
A thousand sheep, as many cows, graze and roam   635
on his ranges; no neighbors hem in his fields.
In his trees with leaves of gleaming, glittering
gold hide golden branches and golden fruit.
"Stranger," says Perseus, "if you're impressed
by brilliant blood-lines, Jove's the source of mine;   640
if it's adventures you like, you'll be awed by mine.
I'd like rest and a place to stay." But Atlas recalls
an old foretelling (Themis of Parnassus told it):
"A day will come, Atlas, that will strip your trees' gold,
and a son of Jove will be famed for the theft."   645
Worried by this, Atlas had walled in his orchard,

set a monstrous dragon to keep it safe,
and held all outsiders well outside his borders.
Now he says, "Go away—or the grand adventures
650   you've made up and Jove himself might fail you."
He adds fist-force to his threats and starts to shove
away this man who tries both sweet-talk and boldness.
At last the weaker of the two (for who's as strong
as Atlas?) says, "Since you welcome me *so* graciously,
655   please accept this gift!" And from the left he thrusts
Medusa's crusted face and turns away his own.
Big as he is, Atlas turns mountain; his beard and hair
thicken to woods; his hands and shoulders, ridges;
what had been head hardens to peak, his bones turn
660   into granite. Now colossal in every way
he scrapes the sky (as you gods decreed), and all
of heaven with its stars rests upon his head.

Aeolus had locked the winds in cratered Aetna,
and the Morning Star, shining deep in the sky,
665   was up to wake the workday, when Perseus tied
feathered sandals to feet, belted on hooking sword,
and, ankle-wings beating, soon split the liquid sky.
He'd left many folk behind, below, and all around,
when he saw Ethiopia and Cepheus' lands.
670   Here an unjust prophet had bid Andromeda
pay—so unfair—for her mother's bold tongue.
The instant Perseus saw her, chained by the arms
to rugged rocks (if a breeze hadn't riffled her hair
and a slow-motion teardrop not rolled from her eye,
675   he'd have sworn she was marble), he inhaled love
unaware and stared, so entranced by the image he saw
that he almost forgot to keep beating his wings.
Hovering near, he said, "Oh, you shouldn't have chains
like those but the kind lovers loop round each other.
680   Tell me, as I'd like to know, your country and name
and why you're in chains." First the girl is silent,
doesn't dare speak to a man, and would hide her face
with her hands if they weren't shackled behind her.
She does what she can: lets her eyes fill with tears.
685   But he presses, and so it won't seem she's unwilling

to spill her own crime, she tells her country and name
and how bold in her beauty her mother had been—
she's not finished talking when the sea suddenly
roars, and from the bottomless deep a monster
rears up and rolls toward them, waves cresting at its chest.   690
The girl screams: at once her grim father and mother
appear, both in despair, the mother more fairly,
but instead of help they bring only tears and wails
that fit the moment and clutch their shackled child.
So the traveler says: "There might be lots of time   695
left for tears, but for helping her time is short.
If I asked for her—I, Perseus, son of Jove
and that towered-up girl he filled with live gold;
I, Perseus, killer of reptile-haired Gorgon,
I who dared unfurl my wings and ply thin air—   700
as suitor, I assume I'm the best. But I'll try
to add service to my endowments (god willing).
My offer: what my bravery saves shall be mine."
Her parents accept his terms (who'd think twice?),
urge him on, and promise the kingdom as dowry.   705

And look—just as a ship's piercing beak slices
the sea when sped forth by men's glistening arms,
so the monster breasts forward, splitting the waves.
It was as far from the cliffs as Balearic slings
can send bullets spinning up into the sky   710
when Perseus suddenly sprang from the ground
and soared into steep clouds. As his shadow dropped
to the top of the sea, the beast struck that shade;
and just as an eagle seeing a serpent sun
its blue-black scales in a lonely field will swoop   715
from behind—lest that hissing mouth lash back—
and will sink greedy claws in the sequined neck,
so Perseus plummeted through empty air,
lit upon the snorting beast, and plunged his sword
into its shoulder clear up to the curving hook.   720
Badly hurt by the stab, the creature thrashed
into the air, plunged underwater, then spun
like a boar ringed by a baying pack of dogs.
Perseus quickly wings free of the snapping jaws

725 and each place he can—barnacle-encrusted back,
ribbed sides, or where dorsal thins into the tail
of a fish—he slashes with his scything sword.
The monster spews seawater sluiced purple
with blood: Perseus' feathers are spattered and sag.
730 With no more faith in his sopping wings, he spots
a craggy rock whose peak juts up when the sea
is still but lurks below when waves are rising.
Perched upon it, clutching a knob, he thrusts his blade
three or four times deep in the beast's tattered gut.

735 Shouts and cheers explode on shore, up to heaven's
halls; Cepheus and Cassiopeia rejoice
and declare Perseus son-in-law, the household's
champion and hero. Now out of chains, the girl
walks forward, reason and reward for his toil.
740 But he's washing his hero-hands in a pail . . .
So the firm sand won't hurt his serpent-clad head,
he makes a nest of leaves strewn with seaweed strands
where he rests the face of Medusa, Phorcos' child.
But a sprig of seaweed—still wet with living pith—
745 on touching the monster feels her power and hardens,
stiffness seeping into the strand's fronds and pods.
The sea-nymphs test the wonder on several sprigs
and are so delighted when it happens again
they throw pods into the sea, sowing seeds for more.
750 And even now this is the nature of coral.
At the touch of air it petrifies: a supple
sprig when submarine in air turns into stone.

He makes a turf altar for each of three gods:
Mercury at left, warrior goddess at right,
755 Jove between the two. For Minerva he kills a cow,
a calf for the wing-foot, bull for the god most high.
Then he takes Andromeda as prize for his deeds,
no further dowry needed. Amor and Hymen
wave wedding torches, sweet oils feeding their flames;
760 garlands dangle from beams; and the air rings
with lutes and singing and flutes, happy themes
of lifted hearts. Then double doors are opened

wide to golden halls, and noble people stream
inside for King Cepheus' glorious feast.
Once they'd all gorged and gotten jolly with wine   765
Perseus asked about the culture and breed
of the place, the habits and thoughts of its folk.
Cepheus told him and then said, "Now, brave boy,   []769
please tell us the talents and tricks you deployed   770
to steal away that head with its shock of snakes."
Perseus told of a place at the foot of icy
Mount Atlas, well fortified by that solid mass.
At its gate lived twin sisters, daughters of Phorcos,
and the two shared the use of a single eye.   775
As they passed it, he stealthily, cunningly, snuck
in a hand and snatched the eye, then carried it off
over far rocky ways stubbled with tree trunks
to reach the house of the Gorgons, passing in fields
and roads along the way figures of beasts and men   780
no longer themselves but stone on seeing Medusa.
Yet *he* saw Medusa's dreadful form only
mirrored in the bright bronze of the shield at his left,
and while she and the snakes were deeply asleep
he swiped the head from her neck: born from her blood   785
were fluttering Pegasus and his brother.
Perseus told the true perils of his long trip,
all the seas and lands he'd regarded from high
and the constellations he'd brushed with his wings.
But sooner than wished he fell silent, so one   790
of the nobles took up the thread, wanting to know
why only one sister had hair tangled with snakes.
The traveler said, "What you ask is worth telling,
so try this account. She was a stunning beauty
once, the greedy ambition of many men,   795
no bit of her more spectacular than her hair—
I heard this from someone who claims he once saw her.
They say the sea-king raped her by Minerva's shrine:
Jove's daughter looked away and hid her pure face
with her shield. So the act would not go unpunished,   800
she turned the Gorgon's hair into hideous snakes.
And even now, to stupefy her enemies,
she wears those serpents she spawned on her breast."

· I . 6

ARETHUSA (5.577–641)

"Once," said Arethusa, "I was one of the nymphs
of Achaea, and no one stalked woods more keenly
than I did; no one was more keen to lay traps.
580   Although I was tough and didn't want to be seen
for looks alone, that's how I was known: my beauty.
But this pretty, praised face of mine did me no good.
Other girls might love it, but I was so country
my lushness made me blush: I thought it wrong to please.

585   "Leaving the Stymphalos woods, I was tired (I recall)
and it was hot, twice as hot for me after hunting.
I came upon a stream with no murmur or whirl,
the water so clear to the bottom you could count
every pebble, as if no current at all.
590   White willows and poplars that the stream sweetly
watered gave back shade to the spring's sloping banks.
I came to the edge and dipped the tip of my foot,
then waded to my knees. Still not content, I pulled
off my soft dress, draped it on a willow bough
595   and plunged nude into the pool. As I slashed and lunged
and glided this way and that, arms slicing the gleam,
I suddenly heard a low murmuring, deep—
and in panic I swam to the nearest bank.
'Where so fast, Arethusa?'—it was Alpheus
600   in his water. 'Where so fast?' he said again, hoarse.
I ran as I was, without any clothes (they lay
on the opposite bank). He chased all the hotter:
because I was nude, I seemed even more prime.
So I ran and he charged behind like a brute,
605   the way fluttering doves might fly from a hawk
and the hawk swoops at those terrified doves.
Past Orchomenos, Psophis, and Cyllene, hollow
Maenalios, cold Erymanthus, and Elis,
I kept running, and he was no faster than me—
610   but I wasn't as strong and could not keep

it up, while he had much more endurance.
Over wide fields and thicketed hills I ran,
past rocks, along cliffs, along no paths at all.
The sun was behind me, his shadow looming
at my feet—unless it was fear that saw this.   615
But the sound of his pounding feet made me numb
and his gusting breath blew hot at my hair.
Nearly fainting from strain, I cried, 'Help me—
Diana—he's got me—your arms-girl, the one
you let carry your quiver, arrows, and bow.'   620
The goddess heard and scooped up some cloud she cast
upon me: the river-god stared at the mist I now
hid in. Baffled, he searched the enveloping fog
around where I stood muffled, and, confounded
he circled me twice and twice called 'Arethusa!'   625
What did it feel like, how horrific? Like
a lamb that hears wolves howling outside her pen?
Or like a rabbit that hides in the shrubs
and sees the dogs' fangs but is too scared to move?
Alpheus stayed put (for he saw no footprints   630
trailing off). He stood and watched my cloud, my spot.
A chill sweat seeped out of my haunted limbs;
deep blue drops slid from all over my skin.
Wherever I stepped turned into pool, dew dripped
from my hair, and faster than I can tell this tale,   635
I'd become a stream. But the river-god knew me
even liquid, shed the man's form he'd assumed, turned
into his water-self so he could flow within me.
Then Diana tore open the earth. I dove through dark
caves and reached Ortygia, which I love because   640
it's Diana's name, too: here I burst into air."

·   I.7

PYGMALION (10.243–297)

"When he saw those women lead such filthy lives
Pygmalion was sickened by the ingrained flaws

245   of the female mind so lived alone, with no wife,
        sharing his bed with nobody for ages.
        But with marvelous skill, he happily carved
        from ivory the form of no woman born—
        and he fell in love with his own creation.
250   It looks like a real girl you'd think is alive
        and longs to be moved, except shyness intrudes—
        art masks his art so well. Pygmalion's in awe;
        flames of love for the feigned body flick at his heart.
        He touches it often with curious hands to see
255   if it's flesh or ivory—it *can't* be ivory.
[]257   He feels his fingers might sink in the limbs he strokes
        and then fears where he's touched might bear a bruise.
        Sometimes he whispers sweetly, sometimes he gives gifts
260   that a girl always likes, shells, polished pebbles,
        tiny birds and blossoms in a rainbow of hues,
        lilies, bright balls, amber drops wept by poplar trees
        that once were Helios' girls. He dresses it, too,
        slips gems on fingers, strands of beads upon the neck;
265   a pearl is fixed to each ear, a corset to breast.
        It all suits her well, but nude she's as lovely.
        He sets her on cushions dyed rich purple of the sea,
        calls her his bedmate, and nestles her neck
        in eiderdown, as if she might actually feel it.

270   "On the holiday of Venus, Cyprus was thronged.
        Heifers with curving gilt horns were dragged inside
        then struck at their snowy necks, and crumpled; incense
        spiraled smoke. Pygmalion gave his gift and stood
        anxious at the altar. 'If you can grant anything,
275   goddess, I wish my wife might be—' he didn't dare
        say *the ivory girl*, instead '—like my ivory.'
        Golden Venus was at the service and divined
        his secret wish: to show that she had nodded yes,
        a flame flared three times, flickered high in the air.
280   At home, he hurried to his modeled girl,
        leaned on the couch, and kissed her: Was she really warm?
        He brushed her lips again and touched a breast;
        where he stroked, the ivory gave, no longer firm
        but soft to his touch, as when Hymettian wax

melts in the sun and, turned about with one's thumb,   285
is molded to forms, more pliable with plying.
Amazed, thrilling nervously, afraid that he's wrong,
again and again the lover strokes what he's wished.
It *is* a live body; veins beat at his thumb!
Then indeed our Paphian hero bursts with words   290
of thanks for Venus and presses real lips at last
with his own. The girl feels the kisses he gives
and goes pink. Then, lifting shy eyes toward the light,
she sees at once both lover and sky.
The goddess was present when they wed, and once   295
the moon's bright horns had filled nine times, the girl
had baby Paphos, who gave the island its name."

II. *Taking*

IO (I.568–746)

There's a gorge in Haemonia wreathed by steep woods;
people call it Tempe. Peneus flows to this gorge
570   from the base of Mount Pindus, rolling frothy waves.
At the falls he lets vapors bloom and shed misty
clouds that fill the woods to the treetops with dew:
from even far afield, the falls' thundering drones.
This is the great river's home, his sanctuary
575   and throne. Sitting in a cave carved from the cliff
he rules his streams and the nymphs dwelling in them.
Here the local rivers have gathered and wonder
if they should applaud or console Daphne's father:
Sperchios lined with poplars, choppy Enipeus,
580   drowsy Apidanos, Amphrysos and Aeas that gleam;
then other rivers who, wherever they wander,
at last lead their weary waters down to the sea.
Only Inachus is missing. Shut in his deep cave
he fills his pools with tears. Broken, he grieves his girl
585   Io is lost. He doesn't know if she's alive
or with the shades, but he can't find her anywhere
so thinks she's nowhere, and he fears yet worse.

Jupiter had seen her walk from her father's banks
and said, "Girl, fine enough for Jove and soon to make
590   some man ecstatic in bed, please stay in the shade
of this deep grove—" (he pointed to the shady grove)
"—while it's so scorching hot, the sun at its height.
If it scares you to go where wild animals lurk,
you'll be safe in those haunts with a guardian god—

and no common god—look, the heavenly scepter   595
is here in *my* hand—I hurl the flying lightning—
don't run!" (She was already gone.) She had left
the Lernean pastures and Lyrcea's woods
when the god cloaked the broad fields in a thick
creeping cloud, caught the girl running, and raped her.   600

Just then Juno happened to glance down at Argos
and marveled that a sudden fog had turned bright day
into night. She knew that this cloud had not risen
from rivers and was not the earth's humid breath.
She looked around for where her husband might be,   605
knowing well the cheating she'd so often caught.
Not finding him in the sky, she said, "I'm either wrong
or being wronged," and she dropped from heaven,
stepped to land, and bid the cloud evaporate.
But he'd had a sense his wife was near and changed   610
Io to look like a luminous cow—
lovely even as heifer. Despite herself,
Juno praised the cow's looks and asked whose she was,
from where and what herd, as if she didn't know.
Jove lied she'd sprung from the soil so her real maker   615
could skirt questions; now Juno wanted her as gift.
What should he do? Giving up his love was cruel;
not giving was suspicious. Shame urged him give,
love urged him not. And love might have beat shame,
but if he refused sister and bedmate a gift   620
like a cow, she might seem to be no cow at all.
So the rival is given, but Juno can't shed
her mistrust and dreads Jove, anxious of more deceit—
so hands her to Arestor's son Argus to guard.

Argus' head was ringed with a hundred eyes,   625
and whenever two of them took turns to nap,
the rest held their posts to guard the young cow.
However he stood, his eyes fixed on Io—
with his back turned, Io was still caught in his gaze.
By daylight he would let her graze, but at dusk   630
he would pen her or unfairly rope her neck.
She feeds on leafy trees and bitter herbs;

for bed she lies on the ground, not always grassy,
poor thing, and the water she drinks is thick with silt.
635   She'd so like to stretch begging arms to Argus,
but she has no arms to stretch to Argus,
and when she tries to wail what comes is a moo.
[]639   She goes to riverbanks where she used to play,
640   the banks of Inachus, but seeing her new horns
reflected she's shocked and shrinks back in fear.

The Naiads don't know her, Inachus does not know
who she is, but she trails father and sisters, lets
them pet her, to their wonder keeps herself still.
645   Old Inachus rips up some grass and holds it out;
she nuzzles her father's hand, kisses his palms,
and can't stop her tears—if words would just come,
she'd beg his help and tell her story and name.
No words—but letters her hoof draws in the sand
650   give the sorrowful sign of her transformation.
"Oh me!" cries Inachus, clutching the horns and
snowy neck of the heifer. She lows and he moans
"Oh me!" again. "Is it really you, my girl I've looked
for all over? You were less painful unfound
655   than found so. You're silent and utter no words
when I speak, but from deep in your heart you heave
such sighs and you do all you can—you moo.
I was stupidly ready for you to wed,
hoping for son-in-law, and grandbabies soon.
660   Now both your mate and young will come from a herd.
And I won't even end these sorrows in death—
oh it hurts to be a god—the door to death
is shut to me and I will suffer on and on."
As he lamented, star-eyed Argus pushed him back
665   and drove Io, torn from father, off to farther
fields. He settled himself on top of a hill
where he could survey in every direction.

Now the ruler of gods can't bear Io's pain
and calls his son, the child of the brilliant
670   Pleaid, and tells him: *Assassinate Argus.*
At once he's got wings on his feet, cap on his head,

and a sleep-stirring wand in his magical hand.
When everything is in place, Mercury springs
from palace to earth. There he takes off the cap
and puts down his wings; all he keeps is the wand.   675
He plays shepherd, leading on country paths some goats
he's charmed along the way by playing his reed pipes.
Juno's guard is beguiled by the curious sound. "You,"
Argus says, "whoever you are, come sit with me
on this rock. You won't find lusher grass for your flocks   680
and you can see that this shade's made for shepherds."
Mercury sits and whiles away the passing day
with talk on many matters, and tries to subdue
those watchful eyes by playing on his reed pipes.
But the other fights to keep from drifting   685
into dreams, and though sleep seeps into several eyes,
the others burn awake. At last (for the reed pipes
are very new) he asks how they were made.

The god began: "In chilly, hilly Arcadia,
among the wood-nymphs of Nonacris was once   690
a most alluring nymph: others called her Syrinx.
She'd slipped more than once from lecherous satyrs
and gods that lurked in teeming fields or twilit
woods. In passions and purity she was like
the Ortygian goddess; dressed as high-skirted   695
Diana she'd fool you and pass as Latona's child,
except her bow was horn and the other's was gold.
No, she'd still fool you. Pan saw her as she walked
from Mount Lycaeus, pine-cone wreath on his head,
and said—" But what he said was still to be told,   700
and how the nymph spun from his proposal and ran
through the wilds until she reached sandy Ladon's
smooth stream; and how, unable to splash across,
she begged that her water-sisters transform her;
and how Pan, when he thought he'd captured Syrinx,   705
clutched no nymphet body but marsh reeds instead;
and how, when he sighed, his breath whistled through
the reeds and made a wisp of sound like weeping;
and how the god was charmed by the new form and sweet

710 note and said, "This will be how we speak, you and I";
and how he joined uneven reeds with ligaments
of wax and named the pipes after the nymph—
Mercury was set to tell all this when he saw
that each eye had sunk to sleep, every light dimmed.
715 At once he hushed and deepened the slumber,
stroking each languid eye with his magical wand.
No time to wait: with scything sword he sliced
the head nodding at the neck and threw it gory
from the rock, blood splashing the rugged cliff.
720 Argus, you lie low. The light once in all your lights
goes out: a hundred eyes eclipsed by one night.
Juno plucked them and scattered them in her bird's
feathers, studded its tail with those gems, star-bright.

But she was on fire and wouldn't temper her rage.
725 She conjured fierce Furies in the eyes and mind
of her Greek foe, planted her heart with blinding
distress, and forced her to wander the world.
Nile, you were the end of Io's grim trail.
As soon as she touched your steep sloping bank,
730 she sank to her knees and threw back her head,
holding up all she could to the stars—her face—
and with groans and tears and mournful moos
she seemed to weep to Jove, beg he end her pain.
He threw his arms around his wife and pleaded
735 that she stop this torment at last. "Don't be afraid,"
he added, "for the future. This one will cause you
no more pain." And he bid boggy Styx take note.
Juno's appeased: the girl resumes her former face
and becomes as she was. Hair falls from her skin,
740 horns wane away, the globes of eyes grow delicate,
the muzzle shrinks, her hands and arms resume their shape,
and each hoof divides into five slender fingers:
no aspect of the heifer remains but a sheen.
Happy now with just two feet, the nymph stands up
745 but is too scared to speak, afraid that she'll still
moo: nervously she utters a few broken words.

◆ **II . 2**

CALLISTO (2.401–507)

Almighty Jove tours the huge walls of sky
to see if the firestorm cracked anything loose
that might fall. Once he sees that all is sound
and safe, he turns to the lands and matters of men.
His Arcadia is what worries him most.   405
He soothes the streams and rivers too nervous still
to flow again, he grasses the fields, and leafs
the trees, and bids the burnt woods green themselves.
As he goes back and forth, he suddenly spots
the girl from Nonacris: warmth flows through his bones.   410
She doesn't care about working wool to suppleness
or deploying different hair styles. A pin fixes
her dress, a white band holds her messy mane,
she always has a bow or spear in her hand:
one of Diana's hunter girls—none on Maenalus   415
makes the goddess more glad. But no power lasts.

The sun was up high and it was just beyond noon
when the girl wandered into a virgin grove.
She slid the quiver from her arm, undid the close-
strung bow, and lay down on the grassy ground,   420
arranging the colored quiver as cushion.
When Jupiter saw her, tired, with no one to see,
"My wife won't notice a little cheating," he thought,
"but if she does—oho, how worth the fight!"
At once he slips on Diana's looks and her gear   425
and says, "Girl, you're one of my company: which hills
did you hunt today?" The girl scrambles from the grass
and says, "Hello, goddess, greater than Jove—and I
don't care if he hears me." He does hear and smiles, likes
being liked more than himself, and kisses the girl—   430
but it's not a quick kiss, no kiss of a virgin.
As she's saying where she hunted, he stops her
with enveloping arms, showing himself and his crime.

She fights against him as much as any girl could
435   (you should have seen her, Juno: you'd be more fair),
she really fights hard, but what man could a girl beat,
and who could beat Jove? Then up to heaven swoops
Mighty Jove; for her—the grove's hateful, the knowing
woods, too. Walking back to her path, she almost forgets
440   to pick up her quiver and darts and bow she'd just hung.

Now here strides Diana across high Maenalus
with her hunter girls, flush with creatures she's killed;
she sees the girl and calls out. But *she* shrinks away,
frightened that Jupiter lurks inside the goddess.
445   Yet when she sees the others coming, too, she thinks
it can't be a trick and adds herself to the troop.
But oh, it's so hard to keep guilt from your face.
She hardly lifts her gaze from the ground, won't
walk with the goddess at the head of her throng,
450   is quiet, her blush telling her hurt and her shame.
If Diana weren't a virgin she would have seen
the signs of guilt. (The nymphs certainly saw them.)
The crescent moon had grown round nine times when
Diana, wan from the hunt and blistering heat,
455   came upon a chill grove where a stream babbled
and runneled as it flowed through firm sandy banks.
A lovely place, she thought, dipped a foot in the spring,
and found it lovely, too. "No one will watch," she said.
"Let's all bathe bare in this gorgeous pool."
460   The Arcadian flushed. The rest pulled off their clothes,
but she put it off, and as she wavered they stripped
her dress away, revealing her body and crime.
Flustered, she tried hiding her belly with her hands,
but Diana said, "Leave at once—do not foul
465   this holy pool," and ordered her out of the troop.

The wife of thundering Jove had known for a while
but delayed her harsh vengeance until time was ripe.
Now no reason to wait: a baby boy, Arcas,
was born to the girl—this alone made Juno rage.
470   She turned on the two her harsh eyes and mind

and said, "Of course that's all that was left, you cheat,
for you to get pregnant and harm me in public,
that child proof of my own and Jove's disgrace.
You won't get away with it. I'll strip the shape
that gave you, rude girl, and my husband such joy."   475
She grips the girl by the hair and flings her down
to the ground. The girl holds up pleading arms—
but they begin to grow shagged with dusky fur,
her hands curve and grow long hooking claws and
really now are feet, the face once so enchanting   480
to Jove becomes an ugly, grisly snout.
So no pleading or prayers could stir any feeling,
her power to speak is taken, too; a rough
growling noise rousing fear rumbles from her throat.
Yet the old thoughts remain inside the new bear,   485
and groaning on end she lifts hands (as they are)
to the sky and the stars to express her despair,
and knows Jove is ungrateful but can't say the words.
So often now she won't sleep alone in the woods
but wanders fields and places that had been her home!   490
So often dogs hound her over rubbled ground
and the huntress scrambles off fearing the hunters!
Seeing a beast she hides, forgetting she *is* one:
the girl-bear shudders to see male bears in the hills
and panics at wolves—though her father lurks among them.   495

Now here comes Arcas, who doesn't know Lycaon's
child—his own mother. He's just turned fifteen.
As he chases wild game and picks the best thickets,
ringing the woods of Erymanthus with nets,
Arcas happens on his mother. She sees him   500
and stops; she seems somehow to know him. But he runs
away from her and those eyes fixed gravely on his,
he's terrified, and doesn't know, and as she nears
and he's poised to drive a ripping spear in her breast—
the Almighty bears them away, and the crime,   505
catches the two in a wind whirling through space
and sets both in the sky as constellations, aligned.

· II . 3

EUROPA (2.833–875)

Once Aglauros had been punished for her words
and nasty thoughts, Mercury sprang from the precinct
835   of Pallas, flung out his wings, and rose to the skies.
There his father called him and said (not admitting
the passion that stirred him), "My boy, you execute
my will so well, quickly slip back down your path
to the land that looks up at your mother's star
840   from the left (the locals call the place Sidon).
Look for the king's cattle—they're grazing near
on the grassy slopes—and drive them down to shore."
No sooner said than cows and bulls were herded
from the mountainside and roaming toward the beach,
845   where the princess played with her Tyrian girlfriends.
Now, love does not go well with dignity or let
it linger long . . . Soon the law-giving god of gods
who holds lightning fire in his fist and with a nod
can shatter the world—he set down his scepter,
850   put on a bull's shape, and mingled with the cattle,
handsome as he ambled, mooing, on tender grass.
He's white as snow that no boots have trampled
and no drizzling warm wind has melted to slush;
his neck swells with muscle, his long dewlap swings,
855   his horns are small, yes, but they seem carved
by hand, more clear and luminous than opal.
His face holds no menace, nothing wild in his eyes:
a look dreamy calm. Agenor's daughter's amazed
that he's so nicely made, no stamping or rage.
860   Although he's tame she's frightened at first to touch,
but steps close, holds buds up to his glistening mouth.
The lover's thrilled: until the craved pleasure can come
he kisses her hands—can hardly wait for the rest!
Now he plays and charges about on the lawn
865   and stretches snow-pure flanks on the golden sand.
Bit by bit, as her fear dissolves, he holds his breast
for girlish hands to pet, his horns to be wreathed

with fresh flowers. The princess even dares climb
the bull's back, no idea who she's really climbing.
And now the god edges from the beach's dry sand,   870
sinking false hoof prints below lapping waves.
Then deeper he goes, taking his prize to the wide
open sea. She's frightened and stares at the shrinking
shore, clutches his horn with one hand and his back
with the other. Her shivering veil flits in the wind . . .   875

❖ II . 4

HERMAPHRODITUS AND SALMACIS (4.285–388)

"Hear how the Salmacis pool got an evil name   285 ◀⁙
for its powerful waters that enervate men.
The potency's famous—the cause, not so known.

"In the caves of Ida, nymphs once nursed a boy,
the child of Mercury and divine Venus.
You could see both mother and father in his face,   290
and his name came from the two of them, too.
When he turned fifteen, he left his mountain home
and the peaks of Ida where he'd grown, eager
to see rivers he'd never seen and go places
he'd never been: excitement sped his feet.   295
He went far—the towns of Lycia and Caria
nearby—and there he saw a still, deep pool,
translucent all the way down. Beside it grew
no marshy reeds, spiky rush, or swamp grass:
its water clear as glass. The pool was rimmed   300
with fresh herbs and moss, bright and ever green.
A nymph lived there, but not one who hunted
or bent a bow or ran hot in the races—
the only nymph quick Diana did not know.
They say her sister-nymphs would often cry   305
'Salmacis, pick up a painted quiver or spear
and have a holiday from lounging, come *hunt*.'
But she'd touch no painted quiver or spear

and take no holiday from lounging to hunt.
310 She just bathed her lovely self in her pond,
often drew a boxwood comb through her hair,
or gazed in her glassy pool to see what looked best.
Sometimes, a see-through dress like light on her skin,
she lay back on the soft silky grass, the soft leaves;
315 often she picked flowers. She was picking flowers
when she saw the boy and wanted what she saw.
She was dying to approach him—but held back
until she'd smoothed her dress and her face, composed
herself, and made certain she was stunning.

320 "Then she went to him and said: 'Boy, oh, you
look like a god, and if so, you could be Cupid . . .
But if you're human—well, your parents are lucky,
your brother's lucky, your sister, if you have one,
is luckier still, and the nurse whose breast touched your lips.
325 But more lucky than they, far more lucky than they,
is the girl you marry, if you've found one to wed.
If you have one, then let my pleasure be secret.
But if not, let *me* be the one: let's go to bed.'
The nymph said no more. But the boy blushed bright
330 (he knew nothing of love). Even blushes became him:
the glow of apples ripening on trees soaked in sun,
or tinged ivory, or the mottled flush of the moon
in eclipse when the cymbals clash in vain.
She kept begging for kisses, a sister's at least,
335 and was circling his ivory neck with her hands
when he said, 'Stop—or I'll leave your place *and* you.'
At this Salmacis panicked and said, 'No, strange boy,
please take the spot,' and turned and pretended to go.
But she kept glancing back, hid in a thicket
340 of shrubbery, and bent down on her knees. Then he,
being a boy and unwatched in the private glade,
danced back and forth, dabbled the tips of his toes
in the lapping pool, dipped a foot to the ankle.
He couldn't wait: lured by the water's light touch
345 he slipped the soft clothes from his slender self.
This really stirred her: the boy's naked body lit
Salmacis with lust. The nymph's eyes glittered
hot, as when the bright burning sun glows back

from a mirror, glows back a brilliant disk.
She can hardly wait, hardly keep back her pleasure,   350
she's wild to hold him, wants so badly she'll burst.
He slaps his body briskly with open palms
and leaps into the pond. Arms stroking in turn
he gleams in that translucent pool like a figurine
of ivory or white lilies encased in glass.   355
'I win him—he's mine!' cries the nymph as she flings
away all her clothes. She plunges into the pool,
clutches the boy as he squirms, forces hard kisses,
and runs her hands over his chest as he writhes,
clinging first to one side of him, then the other.   360
At last she twines about him as he strains to slip
free, like a snake an eagle has snatched and lifts
in the air (dangling, the snake grips the bird's talons
and head, slinking its tail around beating wings),
or like vines that climb trees and smother the trunks,   365
or an octopus entangling the prey it's dragged
deep undersea, its tentacles clasping all over.

"The boy fights hard and won't give up the pleasure
she wants, but she presses so tight she seems sealed
to his skin and says, 'You can fight, nasty boy,   370
but you won't get away. Gods, give me this: let him
never be severed from me, nor me ever from him.'
The gods hear her wish: the two bodies fuse
together and join, one look smoothing over them
both. As when you graft a new sprig to a stem   375
and see the two join and grow together as one—
just like this, as their limbs entangle and meld,
they are no longer two but one doubled form,
not woman or boy: instead neither—or both.
Seeing how waters that were stepped in by a man   380
have engendered a half-man, softening,
Hermaphroditus holds up hands and in a voice
not so deep says, 'Give me this, mother and father,
give this to the child who has both of your names:
let any man who steps into this pool   385
step from it a half-man, made limp by this liquid.'
Both parents hear their biform child's plea
and grant it, tainting that pool with poison.""

· **II . 5**

PROSERPINA (5.346–576)

" 'Sicily is heaped on Typhon's gigantic
limbs, the island's vast bulk pinning him down
because he dared try for a throne in the sky.
Still he keeps straining and striving to rise again,
350   but Cape Peloros pins his right hand, Pachynos
pins his left, while Lilybaeum sits on his legs
and Aetna buries his head. Raging on his back
below, Typhon spews up sand and vomits fire.
He struggles to push himself free of the weight,
355   to roll from his body those mountains and towns—
the earth quakes, and even the lord of the silent
fears that chasms will split open down to the depths
and floods of light will frighten his shades as they shrink.
Alarmed by this threat, the king leaves his shadowy
360   throne, and in his car drawn by sooty black horses
he surveys Sicily's foundations with care.
Once he's explored, found nothing loose, and sets
aside his worries, Venus sees him stroll about
as she lounges on her slopes, winged boy in her arms.
365   "Cupid," she murmurs, "my arms, hands, and *force*—
take those shafts, my child, with which you undo us,
and shoot a swift arrow in the heart of that god
who drew last lot for the three parts of the world.
You tame the gods up here, even Jove; you tame
370   the spirits of the sea and the god who rules them.
Why should Tartarus escape? Why not expand
your rule and mine? A third of the world's at stake.
Even now in heaven (I've stood it so long) we
are disrespected; my influence and yours, Love, wane.
375   Haven't you seen Minerva and lancing Diana
slip from my hands? Ceres' girl, too, will be virgin
forever, if we say yes; she longs to be the same.
On behalf of our alliance—if you care at all—
mate that goddess with her uncle." At Venus' wish

Cupid shakes out his quiver and of the thousand   380
arrows picks one, but there's no arrow more sharp
or precise and none his bow would rather hear sing.
He bends the springing bow at his knee and shoots
a shaft with a hook straight into Dis' heart.

"'Not far from Enna's walls is a lake, a deep lake   385
named Pergus, and not even the Cayster River
has more swans in song on its glossy swells.
Woods wreathe the lake all around, and leafy
boughs ward off the sun's glancing rays like a shade.
Branches shed coolness; the moist earth, fresh buds;   390
here it's always springtime. As Proserpina plays
in this grove, plucking violets and luminous lilies,
tucking them in a basket or folds of her dress,
with girlish intent picking more than her friends—
in a stroke she's seen and wanted and taken by Dis: 395
his desire is pure rush. The frightened young goddess
calls tearful cries to her friends and mother, mostly
her mother, and now she's ripped the top of her dress
the flowers she's gathered fall loose from the folds.
And she's still so young and still so simple   400
that losing her flowers makes her cry all the more.
The thief drives his car onward, shouting and urging
each horse by name and lashing the reins, the dark
rust-red reins, at the horses' manes and necks.
He rides past lakes and the Palici swamps that stink   405
of sulfur and bubble up from cracks in the earth,
and where the Bacchiadae of Corinth—set
between seas—built a city with two different ports.

"'Between Cyane and Arethusa of Pisa
is a small bay enclosed by two narrow capes;   410
Cyane lived here, most famous of Sicilian
nymphs, and the bay has the same name as she.
She rose from the water, stood up to her waist—
and saw and knew the goddess. "No farther!" she said.
"You can't be Ceres' son-in-law by force. The girl   415
must be asked, not taken. If I might compare small
cases to great: Anapis also longed for me,

but I was wooed to wed, not terrorized like she."
Saying this, she stretched her arms wide to block
420   his way. But Dis controlled his temper no more:
he spurred the frothing horses, swung his royal
scepter, and plunged it deep in the pool's sunken
bed. The gouged earth opened a passage to Hades
and took his rushing car deep in her hollows.
425   Cyane mourned the holy girl's theft and her own
say over her pool disdained; in her silent mind grew
an inconsolable wound. Overwhelmed by tears,
she dissolved into waters whose mystic spirit
she'd recently been. You could see limbs go tender,
430   her bones begin bending, her nails growing soft.
Her slimmest parts were the first to turn liquid,
her ultramarine hair, legs, fingers, and feet
(for the slip from slender limbs to cool water
is slight). Then her shoulders, back, hips, and breasts
435   all melted and vanished in rivulets.
At last instead of living blood clear water flowed
through her loosened veins, with nothing left to hold.

"'Meanwhile the girl's frantic mother hunted her
child in every land and each bottomless sea.
440   Neither Dawn as she rose with dripping hair nor
the Evening Star saw her stop searching; she stole
flame from Aetna for torches held in both hands
as she roamed through cold nights, never at rest.
When day came again and faded the stars, she sought
445   her girl, and she sought on from sunset to morning.
She was exhausted and thirsty but had let no
liquid touch her lips when she saw a thatched cottage
and pounded on its little doors. An old woman
appeared, looked at the goddess, and gave the fresh
450   water she asked for, topped with toasted barley.
While the goddess drank, a rough boy with a bold
mouth stood by and laughed and called her greedy.
Insulting! As he mocked she doused the boy with what
she hadn't yet drunk, water, barley, and all.
455   His face drank in the drops as spots, what had been arms
turned into legs, from these new limbs poked out a tail,

and so he wouldn't be dangerous she made him
shrink until he was small and smaller still: a lizard.
As the old woman stared and wept and tried to touch
this marvel, he scuttled to hide. He gained a new name   460
suiting his rudeness, his body starred with spots.

" 'To list each land and sea the goddess roamed
would take so long: there was nowhere left to look.
She returned to Sicily and in her wanders
reached Cyane. If the nymph were not transformed   465
she would tell the goddess all—with no mouth or tongue
she longed to speak yet had no way to do it.
Still she gave a sign by floating on her water's
brim Proserpina's sash, which had slipped undone
into the pool and was one her mother knew.   470
When she saw it, she knew at last that her child
was taken: the goddess tore her tumbled hair
and pummeled and pummeled both breasts with her palms.
What land the girl's in she still doesn't know but blames
them all, calls them thankless, not worthy of her gifts,   475
Sicily the most as it's here she's found proof
of her loss. In rage she smashes plows as they turn
over sods and thus condemns farmers and oxen
to death; she bids the fields betray the hope sunk
inside them by making sure the seeds are spoiled.   480
The fertile lands famous all over the world
now lie racked: at first greening, the wheat withers,
ravaged by too much sun or too much rain
or plundered by bad stars or winds, as greedy
birds peck at the seeds. Darnel and thistle and   485
unprunable weeds strangle the struggling wheat.

" 'Arethusa lifted her head from the Elean
pool, pushed her streaming hair behind her ears
and said, "Oh, mother of fruits and a girl sought
all over the world, stop these long searches   490
and don't be so angry at lands that adore you
and don't deserve this—but were forced open to theft.
I plead not for my own country. I'm here as guest.
Pisa's my homeland; I came here from Elis.

495   I came to Sicily as a stranger but love
       this land the most. It's home to Arethusa now,
       it's where I've settled, so please, sweet goddess, save it!
       Why I left and traveled so many seas until
       I reached Ortygia—a better time will come
500   for my tale, when you're no longer distressed
       and looking more calm. The riddled earth opened
       a passage for me: I swirled through submarine caves
       and lifted my head here to see strange new stars.
       As I flowed underground in the waters of Styx
505   with my own eyes I saw your Proserpina.
       Indeed she looked sad, still some fear in her face,
       but she's a queen, her highness of the shadowland,
       the grand lady of the Underworld's lord."

       " 'At these words the mother froze nearly to stone
510   and for a time seemed stunned. But when awful madness
       was overcome by grief as grave, she took her car
       and flew to heaven. There, her face all storm, hair
       flung wild, she stood before Jupiter full of hate
       and said, "I'm here, Jove, to beg for one who's my blood,
515   also yours. You may not care for her mother,
       but she might move her father, so please love
       her no less because it's I who gave her birth.
       The daughter I sought so long I finally found,
       if you can say *found* to lose her again, say *found*
520   just to know where she is. That she was taken I'll bear
       if he just gives her back; for *your* daughter deserves
       no raiding husband, even if she's no longer mine."
       To which Jove replied: "You and I share the love
       and care of this girl. And if we might call things
525   as they really are, this act is no outrage
       but true love. He'll be no shameful son-in-law
       if you'll accept it, goddess. If he had no more
       how fine to be Jove's brother! But he has far more
       and came after me only by lot. Yet if you must
530   part them, Proserpina may come back to heaven—
       on this condition: that no food down there
       has touched her lips. This, by decree of the Fates."

" 'Now Ceres was certain she'd get back her child.
But the Fates said no: the girl had broken her fast.
Wandering, wondering in the intricate garden   535
she'd plucked a pomegranate from a tilting tree,
split apart the fruit's pale hide, and swallowed
seven seeds. The only one who saw this act
was Ascalaphus, the boy they say that Orphne
(notorious among the Underworld nymphs)   540
bore to Acheron there in his murky woods.
The nasty boy saw and told, so blocked her return.
The queen of Erebus wailed—then made the spy
an unholy bird: just a dash of Phlegethon
and his head grows down, a beak, great glowing eyes.   545
Now he's lost to himself, is folded up in sandy
wings, grows long talons, is all swiveling head,
barely stirs the feathers that fur his former arms.
He's a hateful bird and cries grief soon to come,
the sluggish screech-owl, which always means doom.   550

" 'He might have deserved this for his knowledge
and tongue, but, daughters of Achelous, why do you
have birds' feet and feathers, but faces of girls?
When Proserpina picked her springtime flowers,
were you singing Sirens there, too, with her friends?   555
After you'd combed the world for her in vain
so that the seas would sense your scrutiny, too,
you wished you could skim the water with wings
and your wishes found gods to listen: suddenly
you saw your limbs grow downy gold and feathered.   560
So that your rare singing (which soothes the ears)
not lose the instrument it needs, you've kept
your mouths and tongues: your human voices remain.

" 'Now Jupiter, caught between brother and sister
in mourning, splits the revolving year in two.   565
The goddess's spirit becomes amphibious:
she'll spend six months with mother, six with her mate.
At once there's a change in her thoughts and looks.
The face that had seemed so tragic to Dis

570   is suddenly glad—as when the sun, just covered
        with storm clouds, burns a way through them and out.

        " 'Now gentle Ceres, tranquil with her daughter home,
        asks why Arethusa fled and became a spring.
        The waters grow still as their goddess lifts her head
575   from the depths, wrings her green hair with a hand,
        and starts telling the Elean river's old loves . . . .' "

· II . 6

GANYMEDE (10.143–161)

        Having drawn near him a shady grove, Orpheus
        sat with a council of creatures, tumults of birds.
145   Once his testing thumb had strummed all the strings
        and he'd heard the notes up and down the scale
        ring in tune and harmony, he began to sing:
        "Mother Muse, stir up songs in me from Jove (Jove's
        the source of everything). His power's been my theme
150   before—with somber notes I've sung of Giants
        and shattering bolts shot to the Phlegraean fields.
        But now is time for lighter tones: I'll sing of boys
        great gods have loved and girls stunned by illicit
        lust who deserved what they got for their passion.

155   "The king of gods once fell in love with Ganymede,
        a Phrygian boy, and lit on what he'd rather be
        than Jupiter himself. But he would not turn
        into *any* bird: just one that could fly with his bolts.
        Quick as light he whipped the air with counterfeit wings
160   and snatched away the Trojan boy, who now (though
        Juno hates it) blends Jove's drinks and pours his nectar."

III. *Ruining*

♦ III . I

SEMELE (3.253–315)

The talk goes two ways: the goddess seems too harsh
to some, but others like what she's done, say it suits
her stern virginity; each side argues its case. 255
Only Jove's wife is silent, won't fault or condone
as much as delight in the House of Agenor's pain,
having shifted her hatred of Jove's Tyrian pet
to the girl's household altogether. But now a new
slap: Juno's enraged that Semele swells with mighty 260
Jove's seed. She's whetting her tongue to attack him
then says, "When have my tongue-lashings done any good?
She's the one I'll pursue, it's her I'll destroy, if I'm
really the mighty Juno I'm called, have a right
to my jewel-studded scepter, and am queen and Jove's 265
sister and wife—at least, sister. I bet she likes
quick stolen love: the insult to my bed won't last.
But she's pregnant (now this)—a bulging belly boasts
her crime, and she wants what I've barely had: to be
mother to one of Jove's young. Too bold in her beauty! 270
I'll make it fail. I'm no daughter of Saturn if she
doesn't sink into the Styx, sunk by Jove himself."

She flew from her throne and, cloaked in bright mist, stepped
to Semele's door. Before dissolving the cloud
she made herself old, graying the hair at her brow, 275
dragging lines through her skin, and walking wobbly
and stooped. She made her voice an old woman's, too,

as Beroe, Semele's Epidaurian nurse.
Once they'd been talking a time and finally wound
280   to the subject of Jove, she sighed. "Well, I do hope
it's Jove. But I'm awfully worried: many men
slide into girls' shy beds using the names of gods.
It's not enough to be Jove: he should prove his love
if this really is true. As he is when proud Juno
285   takes him—the exact same size and shape—make him
love you like that, too, decked in all his splendor."
With this talk Juno molds Cadmus' unwitting child,
who asks Jove for a favor, not saying what.
The god says, "Pick anything! I wouldn't say no.
290   So you'll believe me, may the spirit of seething
Styx hear me, too—and that god is every god's terror."
Glad, in trouble, too electric! and soon to die
for his indulgence—she says, "As you are in Juno's
arms when you two play your love games, come to me
295   that way, too." The god wants to stop Semele's mouth
as she speaks, but her quick voice is out in the air.
He moans: she can't unmake her wish, or he unswear
his oath. Deeply sad, he climbs the sloping skies
and with a dark look hauls in mists that stream behind
300   then mixes clouds roiling with sharp flashes and wind
and thunder and lightning bolts no one can flee.
As much as he can, he tries to pen in his strength—
he won't pick up the blazing bolt that atomized
hundred-armed Typhon: that one's too ferocious.
305   There's a more delicate bolt the Cyclops forged
in which he poured less ravaging fury, less fire:
gods call this second-tier arms. With it, Jove enters
the House of Agenor. Semele's body is stormed—
she can't manage this gift and explodes into flame.
310   But her raw little baby is ripped from the womb
and (if you believe it) sewn inside his father's
thigh to fill the time he'd have had in his mother.
His aunt Ino surreptitiously nursed the god-
child in his cradle. Then the nymphs of Nysa
315   hid him in their caves and fed him, gave him milk.

• III . 2

TEREUS, PROCNE, AND PHILOMELA (6.424–673)

Tereus of Thrace routed those ranks with his reserves
and in beating them made a fine name for himself.   425
As he was strong in resources and men and traced
his line back to Mars, Pandion made him an ally
and gave him Procne as wife. But bride-goddess Juno
was not at that wedding, nor Hymen or the Graces.
Furies held wedding torches filched from a grave;   430
Furies laid the wedding bed; a dooming owl settled
on the bedroom roof and brooded in the gables.
That bleak bird when Procne and Tereus married—
that bleak bird when she conceived. Thrace was glad
for them, yes, and they thanked the gods and decreed   435
the day Pandion's daughter married the ruler
and the day Itys was born to be holidays:
benefits can be so well concealed!
                                        Now, the sun
had cycled the years through five falls when Procne,
all coaxing, said to her husband, "If you really   440
like me, please let me go see my sister or let
my sister come to me. You can promise my father
she'll go back home soon. If I could only see her—
you'd give me the greatest gift." So he orders ships
to set to sea and with wind and oar he sails   445
to the port of Cecrops, touching land at Piraeus.
As soon as he's with his father-in-law, hands
are clasped and words are uttered wishing all best.
He begins to say he's come at his wife's behest
and to promise the girl's quick return if she comes—   450
when in walks Philomela, oh, gorgeously dressed,
her own self more gorgeous, as we always hear
Naiads and Dryads look stalking their woods, if
only you gave them the same grooming and polish.
Just seeing the girl, Tereus kindles to fire,   455
as when you touch flame to a cob's shriveled beard

or burn leaves or straw heaped up in a hayloft.
Her looks could well do this, but his natural lust
incites him more, for his breed is quickly aroused—
460   he burns with his own and his people's affliction.
He wants to buy off her caretakers and trusty
nurse, buy her directly with extravagant gifts
and stake his whole kingdom, or why not just *take*
her and keep what he's taken by ruthless war.
465   There's nothing he won't do: he's now so obsessed
with reckless craving, his heart can't tamp the flames.
Barely able to wait, face bright with zeal, he returns
to Procne's request, now pressing his case in her name.
Love lets his words flow, and each time he begs just
470   a little too much, he says it's what Procne wants.
Tears too he produces—as if issued by her!
Oh god, such murky darkness people hide
in their hearts. The effort he puts into evil
makes him seem good, wickedness winning him praise.
475   What, when Philomela wants this as well, wrapping
arms around her father, coaxing—can't she go see
her sister?—pleading for (but against!) her own good?
Tereus watches and prefondles in looking,
seeing her kisses, her arms circling a neck—
480   it all kindles and stirs and flares him up hot.
Each time she embraces her father, he wishes
he were that father (it would be no less obscene).
Her father's won by the pleading. Thrilled, the poor girl
thanks him and thinks it's gone well for both sisters,
485   when soon to both sisters it will bring only pain.

Now Apollo's workday is just about done:
his horses stamp down the wide slopes of sky.
A sumptuous feast is set on the table, wine
in gold cups; at last it's time to drift into sleep.
490   But though he's alone, the Thracian king tosses
and burns, playing again her face, movements, and hands.
What he hasn't yet seen he makes up as he likes—
stirring flames in his mind: there's no chance of sleep.
Now sunrise: Pandion clasps his son-in-law's hand
495   in farewell and, weeping, surrenders his child.

"I give you my girl, dear son, as a good cause compels
me and my girls wish it (as do you, Tereus),
but I beg you—I plead—by your honor, our bound
hearts, and the gods, please treat her with fatherly love
and send back this old man's sweet comfort as soon   500
as you can (it will still seem a long time to me).
Philomela, as soon as you can (bad enough
to miss your sister), be a good girl, and come home."
As he bid all of this, he kissed his child,
and warm tears fell between his words as he spoke.   505
As a pledge of faith he took their right hands,
joined them, and begged they remember to send
his love to his faraway daughter and grandson.
Barely saying farewell at last, he choked
with sobbing and feared the dark dread in his mind.   510
When Philomela's safe on the painted ship   ◀))
and they've shoved off from shore, oars churning the sea,
Tereus cries, "I've won! What I want I now hold."
The brute won't let his eyes ever stray from the girl—   []515
like Jove's hunting eagle that drops in the aerie
the hare it's got trapped in hooked talons—no hope
for the captive: the predator's eyeing his prey.
Now the voyage is done. On shore, they leave behind
the creaky ships—but the king drags Pandion's girl   520
to a shed hidden deep in the old, old forest,
and here, as she turns pale, shakes, is nothing but fear
and asks with tears for her sister, here he locks her,
whispers his unspeakable plan, and rapes her, a girl
all alone, as she helplessly cries for father,   525
for sister, but cries most of all for the gods.
She trembles like a panicked lamb that's ripped but tossed
from a gray wolf's jaws yet still does not seem safe,
or like a dove, feathers slick with her own blood,
that quivers and fears the craving claws that slit her.   530

When she could think again she tore her wild hair
and held out her hands, crying, "Vicious man, brutal,   []533
oh what you've done, no thought for my father's words
or tears, no thought for my sister or me, just a girl,   535
and none for your wedding vows: you care for nothing?

[]539   So no atrocity goes undone, why not kill
540   me too? I wish you had before this unspeakable
act. Then my shade would be immaculate.
But if gods have somehow noticed—if there even
are gods and not everything's died along with me—
one day you'll pay for this. I'll ignore my shame
545   and tell what you've done. If I have the chance
I'll find people and tell. If I'm trapped in these woods
I'll fill the woods and even make the rocks care.
The sky itself will hear me—god, too, if one's there."
All of this churned up the tyrant's brutal rage
550   together with his fear, and maddened by both
he drew the sword from the sheath at his belt,
gripped her hair, twisted her arms behind her back,
and bound her. Seeing the sword, Philomela thrust
out her throat, hoping that she'd die soon; but even
555   resisting and calling again on her father
and struggling to speak, her tongue—he caught it in pincers
and sliced it off with his sword. The tongue's root quivers,
and, trembling and murmuring on the blackened ground—
as when you lop the tail from a snake and it hops—
560   it wriggles and, dying, finds its mistress's feet.
After this horror (I could hardly believe it),
they say he rode her torn body again with his lust.
And then he managed to go home to Procne,
who on seeing him asks for her sister. So he
565   pulls groans from nowhere, tells a tale of made-up death,
with tears to make it true. Procne rips the veil
from her shoulders, a veil glinting with scattered gold,
and shrouds herself in black. She builds an empty tomb,
brings offerings to an absent shade, and grieves
570   the fate of her sister—a fate for different grief.

Now the sun has cycled through the year's twelve signs;
what can Philomela do? A guard blocks her flight,
thick walls of dense rock tower over the shed,
a silenced mouth can give no sign of what's done.
575   But pain is ingenious; sadness breeds brilliance.
On a foreign loom she deftly hangs a web
and on it weaves purple figures in white:

record of her outrage. She gives it to a maid
and bids with hands it reach her mistress. The bidden
woman takes it to Procne, not knowing what she bears.   580
The brutal tyrant's wife unrolls the cloth
and there reads her ruined sister's story—
but (amazingly) says nothing. Fury seals her lips,
and her tongue can't find words raging enough.
No space in her for crying: what's right and wrong   585
explode within, and all she sees is punishment.

Now it's time for women of Thrace to hold Bacchus'
biennial rites. Night knows their holy secrets—
by night Mount Rhodope clashes with cymbals—
at night the queen prepares herself for the sacred   590
mysteries and bursts out, armed and ready to rage.
Her head's tangled with vine, a matted deerskin hangs
at her left, a light spear rests on her shoulder.
With a throng of women Procne storms the woods,
shaking and wild with anger but pretending   595
it's your wildness, Bacchus. She finds the hidden hut
and howls, shouts *Euhoe!* then kicks down the door,
clasps her sister, cloaks her fast in Bacchic
gear and covers her face with leafy vines,
before pulling her, stunned, back to the house.   600

When Philomela sees she's in the monster's home
she shudders, dismayed, her face going pale.
In a safe room, Procne pulls off the sacred gear,
uncovers her poor sister's mortified face,
and wraps her arms around her. But the girl feels   605
like a cheat and cannot look at her sister.
She stares at the ground and wishes she could swear
to god and prove she'd been disgraced by force—
but with no voice, her hands must show this. Procne
simmers with anger she can't contain, stops   610
her sister's tears, and says, "No time to cry.
It's knives we need or something sharper than knives
if you've got it. Sister, I'm ready for any crime:
I'll torch and burn down this palace myself—
I'll throw scheming Tereus into the flames—   615

his tongue and eyes and that part he used to shame
you: I'll cut them off. Stabbing him a thousand times
I'll put out his filthy soul! I'm fully prepared—
for just what, I'm not sure." Procne was running through
620   this when Itys came in, and what she might do
she saw as she stared at him, cold. "Oh, how like
your father you are," she said, and did not go on,
but began to plan the awful act, seething, silent.
But when the child went to his mother to murmur
625   hello, twined his small arms around her neck,
and gave her kisses and little-boy whispers,
her mother-self melted, her loosened rage slipped,
her helpless eyes pooled and then streamed with tears.
When she saw her mind shift with too much affection
630   she turned again to face her sister, looked from one
to the other. "Why should one sweetly whisper,
while the other be mute, tongue ripped from her mouth?
He can say *mother*, but she can't say *sister*?
You daughter of Pandion: see what you've married.
635   You degrade us. Faith to Tereus is a sin."

At once: she pulled Itys away, as a Ganges
tiger drags a milk-mouthed fawn in shadowy woods.
When they reached a hidden quarter of that proud house,
even as he saw what she'd do, held out his hands,
640   cried, *Mother, Mother*! and clutched at her neck,
Procne stabbed a knife in her son where side meets chest
and did not turn her face. This stab was enough
to kill the boy, but Philomela slit his throat,
and they cut up the body still trembling with breath
645   and warm. Some pieces bubble in deep bronze pots;
others sizzle on spits; the room is smeared with filth.
To this meal witless Tereus is called by his wife.
She lies that it's a grave family practice—only
husbands can come—and sends away his company.
650   So Tereus sits high on his ancestral throne
and feeds, stuffing his belly with his own, his son.
So much darkness in his soul—"Fetch Itys," he says.
Procne can no longer hide her bitter delight;
wanting to announce her ruin herself, she says,

"You have what you want right there." He glances about,   655
looks for the boy; and as he looks and calls again,
just as she is, hair spattered from savage slaughter,
in bursts Philomela. She throws the boy's bloody head
at his father's face, and she's never wanted so
much to speak, to find the right words for her joy.   660
With a roar the Thracian shoves the table away
and shouts to the snaky sisters of underland Styx.
First he's crazed and would if he could slit open his gut,
dig out the hideous meal and half-eaten flesh;
then he weeps and says he's his boy's tragic tomb;   665
now with bare sword he hunts Pandion's daughters.
But the sisters suddenly seem fluttering, feathered:
they do flutter with feathers! One flies to the forest,
one up to the roof, and on their breasts they still bear
the markings of murder: plumage speckled with blood.   670
And he in his rage and rushing lust to avenge
becomes a bird, too: on his head stands a crest
and his oversized beak juts out like a sword.

· III . 3

SCYLLA (8.6–151)

Meanwhile Minos besieged the Megaran coast
by testing his strength on the town of Alcathous.
It was ruled by Nisus, who had in the whorling
white hairs on his head a single sea-snail purple
lock: the key to his kingdom's security.   10
By now the sixth crescent moon had risen and waxed
but still the war's outcome wavered, as Victory
flitted to one side, fluttered back to the other.
A royal tower rose from the town's singing walls—
singing, as Apollo had slipped inside the stones   15
a golden lute whose sound still strummed within.
Nisus' daughter would often climb those steep steps
and aim a small pebble at the stones that sang,

at least in days of peace. She would climb the steps
20   in wartime too, but to watch the bitter battles.
By now she knew the rules of war, the princes' names,
arms, horses, and colors, and the Cretan quivers.
She knew best how the general, Europa's son, looked:
she knew this way too well. She thought if Minos
25   had on his head a crested helmet with a plume
he was handsomest in a helmet; if he slung
on his arm a bright bronze shield, shields became him best;
if he flung a thick javelin, muscles strained taut,
the girl praised his talent so sinewed with strength;
30   if he bent broad his bow, arrow tightly in place—
surely Apollo stood just so with his shafts.
But when he threw back the visor to bare his face
and, caped in purple, rode his white horse saddled
with bright tapestried cloths and reined its foaming mouth—
35   then oh then could Nisus' daughter barely think,
barely keep hold of herself. Oh, how lucky the spear
he touched, how lucky the straps tight in his hand!
If she could, she was dying to wend a delicate
way through enemy lines, dying to cast herself
40   from this high, high tower into the Cretan camps,
throw open the bronze doors, ask the enemy in,
and do anything else Minos liked.
                              She pondered
as she gazed down on the Cretan king's white tents:
"To be sorry or glad for this grim war I don't
45   know: it hurts that Minos my love is the enemy,
but without war I would never have known him.
Yet if he took me as hostage he could cut short
this war; in me, he'd have a pledge of peace.
If your mother was like you—you most fabulous
50   creature!—no wonder that god adored her.
Oh I'd be happy times *three* if I could wing
through the air to the Cretan king's camp,
and tell him I love him—oh—ask what he'd take
for me—but he'd better not ask for our city.
55   Better my honeymoon hopes dissolve than I win
what I want by treason, though an especially kind
conqueror can make it not bad to be conquered . . .

Besides, his war's righteous: for his murdered son.
Since he's reinforced by both army and cause,
I think we'll fall. If this is what awaits our town,   60
why should his war-power lay open our gates
rather than my love? Better that he overtake
us without slaughter, suspense, or spilling his blood.
Then, Minos, I wouldn't fear someone might stupidly
wound you; for who could be such a brute he'd dare   65
throw a cruel spear at you, unless by mistake?
I like this plan: I move that I deliver myself
with my country as dowry and end this campaign.
But *wanting* won't do. A guard watches the portal;
my father holds keys to the gates. Oh, it's only   70
him I fear; he alone can block what I want.
I wish to god I had no father! We're each our *own*
god, really. Fortune's disgusted by lazy desire.
Any other girl burning like this would have long
since demolished whatever hindered her love.   75
Why should anyone be tougher than me? I'd walk
through fire or run on blades—but here neither fire
nor blades are the issue; the issue's my father's hair.
To me it's more precious than gold: that purple lock
will make me so glad—able to grant my *own* wish."   80

Nighttime, sweet healer of worries, slowly sank
as she pondered, and darkness swelled her daring.
It was early and still, when sleep seeps into souls
worn down by daily worries. She stealthily stole
to her father's room and (outrageous!) cut off   85
his crucial lock. With this appalling prize in hand,
she strode (sure of her worth) through enemy lines   []88
to the king, the horrified king, and she said,
"Love's made me do this. I'm Scylla, royal child   90
of Nisus, and I give you my home and land.
The only prize I want is you: as pledge of love
take this purple lock, and know I give you not just
hair but my father's head." With scandalous hand
she held out her gift—but Minos recoiled,   95
repelled by the sight of her radical act.
"May gods rid this world of you, almighty horror,"

he said, "and may you be chased off land and sea.
I would never let such a monster touch Crete,
100   the cradle of Jove and whole world to me."
And once the righteous leader had laid down laws
on the people he'd conquered, he bid his men
unmoor the fleet and row bronze-sheathed ships to sea.

When Scylla saw the ships untied and set afloat
105   and the general paying no prize for her crime,
she begged all she could—and then shifted to rage.
Hair wild, hands outflung, brain on fire, she screamed
"Where do you run, deserting her who let you win,
who favored you over fatherland—and father?
110   Where do you run, you harsh man, when your conquest
was my crime and my service? Not my gift or love
or the fact that I set all my hopes on just
you—nothing moves you? Deserted, where do I go?
Home? It lies in ruins. But imagine it there:
115   my betrayal locks me out. To face my father?
I surrendered him to you. Our people hate me;
our neighbors fear my example. I've shut myself
from the world, so Crete is my only option.
If you bar it too, thankless man, and leave me,
120   no Europa bore you, but hard-bitten Syrtis—
Armenian tigers—swirling, torrid Charybdis.
You're not Jove's son: no fantasy bull ever tricked
your mother (the family tale's a lie): it was
[]125   a *real* bull that spawned you. Exact your punishment,
Papa Nisus! Be thrilled by my troubles, you walls
I betrayed! I admit I deserve and ought to die.
But let someone I've shamelessly hurt get to kill
me. Why should you both profit from and prosecute
130   my crime? Let my offense to father and land
be just a favor to you. She really is the mate
for you, that cheat who tricked a raging bull with wood
and bred a mongrel in her womb. Do any words
reach your ears, thankless man, or does the wind bear
135   away my useless voice as quickly as your ships?
[[]]138   Oh god! He's ordered them to lean in hard and chop
the sea—it roars—and my land and I will vanish.

You'll get nowhere ignoring my favors in vain.   140
I'll follow despite you—I'll clutch the curved stern
and ride the wide seas." And she leapt into the waves
and swam after the fleet, racing with passion,
then like a parasite clung to the Cretan ship.
When her father saw (he was a sea eagle now   145
and coasted the wind on his new umber wings),
he swooped to rip her with a hooked beak as she hung.
In terror she let go the stern—but a light breeze
seemed to hold her fall, not let her touch the sea—
there's a feather, more feathers—and now she's a bird!   150
She's called Ciris: a new name for her shearing.

·   III . 4

HYACINTH (10.162–219)

"Apollo would have set you in heaven, too,
Hyacinth, if bitter Fates had given him time.
But in a way you live on: when spring melts the ice
and Aries takes water sign Pisces' place in the sky,   165
you rise again from your green bed and bloom.
My father preferred you above all, and Delphi
(the world's center) did without its resident god
while he hung near Eurotas and unfortified
Sparta. He cared no more for his arrows or lute: 170
forgetting himself, he'd agree to haul in nets
or hold back dogs or hike as your comrade up steep
mountain slopes; by nearness he nurtured his passion.

"The sun was high, almost midway from daybreak
to dusk, hovering halfway through the sky.   175
The two stripped off their clothes, slicked their skin with sleek
olive oil, and set off to compete with the discus.
Apollo cast first: his disk soared into transparent
air until it had plumbed the shadowing clouds.
After a time the weight plummeted back to firm   180

earth, showcasing his skill so sinewed with strength.
But the Spartan boy—unthinking, eager to play—
had leapt at once to fetch the disk, and the hard
ground cast it bouncing back so it struck him,
185   Hyacinth, in the face. The god went as pale
as the boy himself and clasped his crumpled limbs.
He tried rubbing him warm, tried staunching the gash,
tried to stopper with herbs the spirit slipping away.
But his skills did no good: the wound couldn't be healed.
190   As, in a fresh garden, you snap stems of violets
or poppies or lilies with long golden tongues
and they wilt and soon droop their heavy, creped heads
and can no longer stand but gaze at the ground:
so, as he died, his face was cast down and his neck,
195   with no strength for itself, slumped down to his chest.
'You slip away, Hyacinth, cheated while young,'
cried Apollo, 'and your wound is my crime, I know.
You're my heartbreak and error; my right hand ought
to be branded for murder—I'm your cause of death.
[[[]]202   Oh, I wish I could give up my life either for you
or with you! But since we're trapped by laws of fate,
you'll live only by lingering on my haunted lips.'
[[[[]]]]209   Even as Apollo (who tells the truth) is speaking—
210   look! The blood that spilled and stained the grass is no
longer blood: a flower brighter than Tyrian
purple springs up and looks like a lily except
that it's purple while lilies glow silvery white.
But Apollo (source of this honor) isn't done yet:
215   he prints his sad cries on the petals—*AI AI*—
these mournful letters are drawn on the flower.
And Sparta's not sorry it bore Hyacinth
but honors him still, holding the Hyacinthia
as in years past, days marked with pomp and parade."

• III . 5

ADONIS (AND ATALANTA) (10.503–739)

"The baby that was so darkly conceived grew
inside its mother's bark until it sought a way
free; on the trunk, a belly knob, swollen.   505
The pressure aches, but Myrrha's pain has no words,
no *Lucina* to cry as she strains to give birth.
As if truly in labor the tree bends and moans
and moans more, the bark wet with sliding tears.
Then kind Lucina comes and strokes the groaning   510
limbs, whispering words to help the child slip free.
The bark slowly cracks, the trunk splits, and out slides
the live burden: a baby boy wails. Naiads set
him on silky grass, wash him with his mother's tears.
Even Envy would call him lovely: the naked   515
cherubs you see in paintings—just like one of them.
But in case their trappings let you tell them apart,
take away their light quivers, or give one to him.

"Time glides by in secret, so swift we can't see:
nothing's quicker than years. That child of his own   520
grandfather and sister, first hidden in a tree,
then born, and then the most lovely baby,
is now boy, now man, now more lovely than himself.
He pleases Venus, too, pays back his mother's flames.
For as the boy with arrows gives his mother a kiss,   525
by mistake an arrow peeks out, grazing her breast.
The goddess is stung and thrusts him away; the cut
is deeper than it seems, and she herself is fooled.
Undone by a man's beauty, she stops attending
Cythera's beaches, won't go to Paphos edged by sea,   530
fish-filled Cnidos, or Amathus laden with copper.
She stays far from heaven—heaven, if there's Adonis?
She holds him, clings close, and though she usually stays
in the shade to nourish her beauty with tenderness,
now she hikes over ridges, in woods, through brambles   535

and rocks, her dress hiked to the knees like Diana.
She goads the dogs and drives out any creatures
safely ensnared, mad-dash hares and deer and stags crowned
with antlers, but she stays away from fierce boar
540 and very far from slavering wolves, saber-clawed
bears, and lions all sopped in cow blood.
She warns Adonis, too, to scare him—as if warning
has ever done good. 'Be bold with beasts that bolt,'
she says. 'It's not safe to be brave with the brave ones.
545 Please don't be rash, boy, and put *me* in peril;
don't stir up the beasts that nature's heavily armed
and let your glory cost me. Your beauty and youth
and all that move Venus won't move lions one bit.
[]550 Wild boar with those tusks strike violent as lightning,
the rush of tawny lions is ravage and rage—
I hate the entire species.' Oh, why? 'I'll tell you,'
she says. 'You'll marvel at an old crime's odd outcome.
But all that unnatural work has tired me—look!
555 A poplar luring with shade when we want it, a lawn
forming a love seat. I'd *love* to lie down' (she does)
'here with you,' and she settles on grass and Adonis.
Leaning back, she nestles her head in his young lap
and tells a story, mingling her words with kisses:

🔊560 " 'You might have heard of a girl who always beat
the fastest men in races. The talk was no tale:
she really did win. And you couldn't quite say
if she shone more for her famous feet or fine looks.
She asked a seer about marriage: "Marriage," he said,
565 "you don't need. Run away from the habit of marriage.
No: you won't run away; you'll lose yourself, still alive."
Frightened by this fate, Atalanta dwells unwed
in thick-set woods, fends off urgent throngs of men
with a dangerous condition: "I won't be had
570 unless beaten in a race. So race with me," she says.
"The prize for speed will be a warm wife in her bed;
second place gets death. These are the rules of the game."
She's certainly severe. But (her beauty's so strong)
nervy throngs of lovers hurry even at these terms.
575 Hippomenes sat in the stands of one tilted race

and said, "Who's willing to risk so much for a wife?"
He disdained those other boys' excessive desire.
But when he saw her face and—robe dropped—her shape
(which was like mine, or like yours, if you were a girl),
he was stunned. Raising his hands he said, "Pardon me,   580
all those I judged; I had no idea of the prize
you sought." As he appraises, love's lit inside.
He hopes that no boy can run faster than she can
and fears that one might play a trick. "But why
don't I try my luck in this contest?" he thinks.   585
"God helps those who dare things." As Hippomenes
ponders, the girl streaks by as if she's winged.
Although it seems to him she flies as fast as
a Scythian arrow, her beauty amazes
him even more, and running blooms her beauty.   590
Wind streams like feathers from her flying feet;
her hair tosses and whips on her gleaming back;
from her legs flit the colored fringes of knee bands.
A flush runs over the girl's pearly skin,
as when a red awning over a marble hall   595
suffuses it with the illusion of hue.
As the boy watches, the last post is passed:
Atalanta wins and is crowned with a wreath
and the beaten boys, groaning, pay the price.

" 'Not put off by how it had turned out for them,   600
Hippomenes stands and looks the girl in the face.
"Why chase an easy win by beating worthless boys?
Race with me," he says. "If luck lets me win, to be
beaten by *me* won't embarrass you. My father's
Megareus of Onchestus; his grandfather's   605
Neptune: I'm great-grandson of the king of the sea,
and *I'm* just as strong as my bloodline. If you win,
you'll win a fine name for beating Hippomenes."
As he talks, Atalanta gazes with dreamy
eyes and wonders if she'd rather win or be won.   610
"What god," she thinks, "so jealous of beautiful boys
wants him to die, making him risk his sweet life
for a wife? In my opinion—I'm not worth it.
I'm not touched by his beauty (yet could be), but that

615 he's still a boy. *He* doesn't move me; his age does.
What of his courage, this soul not scared of death?
What of his being four generations from the sea?
What of his loving me and so prizing wedding me
that he'd die if bad luck won't let him *have* me?
620 Strange boy, run from such bloody bonds while you can.
Marriage—mine—is bitter. Who wouldn't want to wed
you? Of course you'll be chosen by some clever girl.
But why worry for him, given all those who've died?
He can look out for himself! Let him die if he's
625 not scared by such slaughter; he must be sick of life.
So, he'll die because he longed to live with me,
a lowly death will be his reward for love?
And if I win it'll bring me nothing but hate.
But it's not my fault. I wish you'd forget this,
630 or, if you're so foolish, I wish you'd be fast!
But what a girl-like expression in that boy's face . . .
Oh, Hippomenes, you should never have seen me.
You deserved to live. But if I were more lucky
and troublesome Fates didn't keep me from wedding,
635 you're the one I'd have most liked in my bed."
So naive—her first desire! Without knowing,
she's fallen in love, with no idea what love is.

" 'Her father and the townsfolk had called for the race
when Neptune's boy Hippomenes called upon *me*
640 and he sounded distressed: "May Venus please be near
me in this riskiness, please fan the love she's lit."
A fair breeze blew his sweet prayer my way, and I
must say I was moved but had little time to help.
There's a meadow the locals call Tamasus,
645 the best land in Cyprus. Ages ago the elders
consecrated it to me and bid its riches
flow to my temples. In this field blooms a tree—
golden leaves, branches rustling with glowing gold.
I'd just stopped by and had in my hands three
650 golden apples I'd plucked. Seen by no one but him
I went to Hippomenes and showed what to do.
Then the trumpets blared: from the starting gate the two
sprang forth, flashing feet barely brushing the sand.
They could skim the sea without wetting their toes

or race atop tips of grain ripening in wheat fields.   655
The roar and cheers spurred on the boy, the shouts
and hoots from the sidelines: "Now pick up your speed,
Hippomenes, run! Give it your all—don't let up
and you've won!" Who knows if Hippomenes
or Atalanta was happier to hear this?   660
Oh, how often when she could pass she paused,
gazed long on his face, pulled away so reluctant!
His mouth fallen slack, he panted parched breath,
but the finish line was far away—so at last
Hippomenes tossed one of his three apples.   665
The girl was surprised and liked the bright fruit
so turned to follow the gold as it tumbled.
Hippomenes passed: the bleachers roared with applause.
Back on track quickly, she made up for the pause
and distance she'd lost and left the boy behind.   670
But then the second apple was tossed—she fell back,
then chased and passed him again. Last stage of the race
to go. "Be here," he said, "goddess, who granted this gift,"
and he wildly hurled the gleaming gold to a far
part of the field—it would cost her time to get it.   675
Whether to chase she didn't seem sure, so *I* made
her fetch it and made denser the apples she held,
hindering her equally in weight and in time.
So my story won't be more slow than the race,
the girl was outrun; the winner led off his prize.   680

" 'Adonis, didn't I deserve thanks and the honor
of incense? But he was oblivious—no thanks
and no incense. All at once I was pure rage,
stung by his contempt, and so I'd not be scorned
again I chose to make of the two an example.   685
They were passing a temple bright Echion built
to thank Cybele, a temple deep in leafy
woods, and their long journey urged them to rest.
But here a sudden wild lust to sleep with his wife
came over the boy—roused by *my* mystic will.   690
Near the temple was a grotto, dimly lit
and like a cave carved from volcanic rock,
a holy place for primitive rites where a priest
had gathered wooden figures of the ancient gods.

695   Hippomenes entered this place: he spoiled it with lust.
      The holy figures looked away, and tower-topped
      Cybele was set to plunge the two in the Styx
      but the sentence seemed too light. Instead their necks
      grew furred with manes, their fingers curved to claws,
700   their upper arms thickened to shoulders, all their weight
      swelled into their chests, and tails now swept the sand.
      Their faces savage, instead of words they rumble roars,
      instead of rooms they roam the woods arousing fear
      but, fangs restrained, they strain Cybele's reins, as lions.
705   Now you, my love, stay clear of them and any beast
      that doesn't turn its back to run but bares its chest
      to fight, or your boldness might ruin us both.'

      "Venus warned him, then sailed away in the air
      on harnessed swans. But brave boys shrug at warnings.
710   His dogs had followed the tracks of a wild boar
      to its den and provoked it: now it stormed the woods,
      and Cinyras' boy pierced it with a slanting thrust.
      The crazed boar briskly shook the blood-spattered spear
      from curving snout and charged Adonis—who panicked
715   and scrambled to hide—then sank its tusks in his groin
      and left him sprawled in the yellow sand to die.
      Venus was coasting in her light swan-drawn car
      and she hadn't yet gotten to Cyprus, but
      hearing the far groans of her boy as he died,
720   she wheeled her white birds around. As she saw
      from the sky him lying and dying in blood,
      she leapt down at once, tore her clothes and tore
      her hair and beat both breasts with brutal hands.
      Wailing at the Fates, she said, 'Not everything's
725   in your command: a memento of my grief will live,
      Adonis, always. Yearly miming of your death
      shall bring yearly echoes of my sorrow.
      Your blood shall be a blossom. If Proserpina
      changed a young girl into fragrant mint, will I
730   be grudged the transformation of my hero,
      Cinyras' boy?' And saying this, she sprinkled
      scented nectar on his blood. With every drop
      the blood began to swell, as when bubbles rise

in volcanic mud. No more than an hour had passed
when a flower the color of blood sprang up,   735
the hue of a pomegranate hiding ruby seeds
in its leathery rind. But the pleasure is brief:
the anemone barely clings and falls at a breath,
shaken free by the wind that lives on in its name."

· III . 6

GLAUCUS AND SCYLLA (13.898–14.69)

Galatea falls silent; with their circle dissolved
the Nereids scatter and swim the smooth waves.
Not Scylla, though (she doesn't dare swim in deep   900
seas). She wanders undressed on the thirsty sands
or, if she feels wan, finds hidden caves of swirling
surf and cools her body in the watery coves.
Now look—a new sea creature's cleaving the waves:
Glaucus, only newly transformed, near Anthedon   905
in Euboea. On seeing the girl he lingers,
longing, and calls out words he thinks might make
her stay. But all the same she bolts, afraid,
and quickly climbs a cliff that juts above the shore.
It's a crest that overlooks the beach and towers   910
to a tree-topped peak that arches over the sea.
Here she stops—it's surely safe—and wonders whether
he's monster or god: his color is amazing,
and the hair flowing over his shoulders and back,
and those lower loins that twist into a fish.   915

When he spots her, he leans on a rock and says
"I'm no freak or animal, girl, but a sea god,
and not Proteus or Triton or Athamas'
son Palaemon has more marine might than me.
I used to be human, but, it's true, addicted   920
to ocean, for my work was with the sea.
Sometimes I'd pull in the nets that pulled in fish,

or, perched on a rock, I'd handle rod and line.
There's a beach that's bordered by a green field,
925   one side fringed with sea foam, the other with grass,
which no horned cow has ever ripped or chewed,
and no peaceful sheep or shaggy goat has cropped;
no buzzing bee has drawn from its blossoms,
it's opened flowers for nobody's wreath, and no
930   hand with a scythe has slashed it. I was the first
to sit on that grass as I dried my dripping lines
and laid out the fishes I'd caught to count them,
fishes that either chanced into my net
or whose gullibility led to my hook.
935   It's like a story (but why tell a tall tale?):
upon touching the grass my catch starts to twitch,
to flip and squirm into soil as if in the sea.
I sit there stunned as my flock flits to the waves,
leaving its new home, the shoreline, deserted.
940   Astounded, I ponder how this can be:
was it done by some god or a juice in the grass?
But what herb could have such potency? I rip
up a green handful and chew what I've ripped.
My throat barely swallowed the mysterious juice
945   when suddenly I felt my heart wriggle inside—
my breast rushed with love for a new nature: sea.
I couldn't wait and cried, 'Farewell, land—I won't
be back!' and plunged myself into the surf.
The sea gods considered me fit for their ranks
950   and asked Oceanus and Tethys to strip
my recent mortality. They cleansed me and sang
a sin-purging charm around me nine times,
then bid me bathe my chest in a hundred streams.
At once rivers that tumbled from each point
955   of the compass poured waters over my head.
This much I can tell you of what I recall;
this much I remember; my mind lost the rest.
When my wits returned, I found my body not
what it had been, and my mind was altered, too.
960   It was then I first saw my dusky green beard
and the maning hair I sweep over the swells,
plus my massive shoulders and these sky-blue
arms and legs that now curve into finned fish.

But what good are my looks, or pleasing the sea gods,
or *being* a sea god, if none of this moves you?"   965
For Scylla's already run from the god as he talks
and is set to say more. Lit to rage by rejection,
he seeks Sun-daughter Circe's fabulous halls.

Glaucus plowed the swollen seas and left behind   14.1
Aetna heaped upon Typhon's gigantic throat
and the Cyclops' lands that have felt neither rake
nor hoe and owe nothing to teams of oxen.
He left Zancle, the facing walls of Rhegium,   5
and the shipwrecking straits that cut Ausonia
from Sicily and give each land its edge.
Stroking hard through the Tyrrhenian Sea,
he reached Sun-sprung Circe's botanical hills
and her halls—her menagerie of beasts.   10
When he saw her and they'd traded hellos,
he said, "Goddess, I'm begging you: pity a god.
Only you, if I'm worth it, can lighten my love-pain.
The power of drugs—no one knows better than I
do, Titania, given that they transformed me.   15
So that you'll know what's making me senseless:
on the Italian shore, facing Messene's walls,
I saw a vision: Scylla. I'm pained to tell my vows
and fawning words and pleas—all of them rejected.
But you: if charms can change things, chant a charm   20
with those holy lips; if a potion's more potent,
use guaranteed doses of most magical herbs.
I don't ask you to cure me or heal these wounds
(I don't want to end this!): I want *her* burning, too."

To this Circe said (for no one's more instantly   25
love-lit than she, whether it's truly her nature
or stems from Venus, mad at the Sun for spying):
"Better to chase someone who wants and longs
for the same as you, someone likewise in love.
You should have been chased (and you still could be);   30
if you gave someone hope, believe me, you would be.
Don't be uncertain—have faith in your looks.
For though I'm a goddess, the glowing Sun's child,
and can do as I like with charm words and herbs—

35   I'd love to be yours. Scorn her who scorns you; want
      her who wants you: in one step you'll repay us both."
      But to such seductions Glaucus said: "Trees will grow
      in the sea and seaweed on mountains sooner
      than my love will change, as long as Scylla lives."

40   The goddess was furious, but couldn't harm
      him (a lover just can't), so fixed her fury
      on the one he preferred. Stung her love was disdained,
      she ground foul grasses with hideous liquors,
      then mashed and mixed them with Underworld chants,
45   draped herself in airy blue, stalked through her throng
      of slavering animals and out of her hallways,
      then, heading for Rhegium near the Zancleian
      rocks, she sped over tossing, tempestuous waves
      and strode sea as though she paced on firm land,
50   skimming the billowing surf with dry feet.

      There was a small pool that scalloped and curved,
      a quiet place Scylla was glad for. Here she'd hide
      from roiling sea or sky when the sun was too hot
      as it hung so high and cast so little shade.
55   With preternatural potions Circe poisons
      this place: she drips oils squeezed from toxic roots
      and murmurs spells of strange and murky circling
      words nine times, times three, with her witchy lips.
      Now Scylla appears: she dips herself to the hips
60   and suddenly sees her loins deformed to barking
      beasts. At first she can't believe these creatures are *her*,
      tries to get away—or get *them* away—afraid
      of the snapping jaws. But what she flees follows,
      and as she flails for her body—thighs, shins, or feet—
65   she touches the fangs and muzzles of hell-hounds.
      She stands amid raving dogs that once were her hips,
      struggling to tame the wild bodies beneath her.

      Glaucus wept for the girl he'd loved, and he kept far
      from Circe, too cruel with her powerful potions.

IV. *Wanting Someone too Close*

· IV . I

BYBLIS AND CAUNUS (9.454–665)

Byblis is proof that girls ought to love lawfully,
Byblis, who fell in awful love with her brother.   455
At first, it's true, she can't understand her desire   []457
or see that it's wrong to keep kissing him so,
twining her arms around her own brother's neck:
she's fooled by what seems to be sisterly fondness.   460
But bit by bit her love sinks: she goes to him dressed
for his eyes alone, wants so much to seem lovely
that if anyone seems more lovely—is jealous.
Still she can't see what she does and hasn't yet hoped
for anything more: but inside she's starting to smoke.   465
She starts calling him *sir*, hates her family name,
and wants him to call her *Byblis*, not sister.
Unspeakable fantasies haven't yet wormed
in her conscious mind, but in dreams she sees
what she wants: visions of her limbs entangled   470
with his—and she blushes even while sleeping.
Sleep drifts away, but she lingers in bed, replays
what she's seen. Her thoughts disarrayed, she thinks
"Oh god—what can this silent dream be about?
I would *never* want that. Why have these visions?   475
Yes, he's gorgeous and allures even those who don't
like him; if he weren't my brother, I could love him,
he's worth it—oh, being his sister does me no good.
But if I never try anything while I'm awake,
may sleep often slip me these marvelous dreams . . .   480
There's no pleasure missing—and no one to see.
Oh, Venus, with winged Cupid beside you,

how glorious it was! I really *felt* desire
overwhelm me! I seemed to dissolve to my core.
485   Just recalling it's thrilling, even if joy was brief
and the night raced by, jealous of what we'd begun.
Oh, if I could just change my name and be with you,
Caunus, how fine a daughter I'd make your parents!
Caunus, how fine a son you would make *mine*!
490   The gods could let us share everything except
grandparents: I'd want you better born than I.
Beautiful boy, you'll make some no one a mother;
for me, who sadly got the same parents as you,
you'll only be brother. We're blocked by what we share.
495   But what do these dreams mean? Exactly what substance
do dreams have? Do dreams even have any substance?
God forbid! Yet even gods have had their sisters . . .
Saturn took Ops, who was family by blood;
Oceanus took Tethys; Jupiter, Juno.
500   But gods have their own laws. Why try to compare
human habits with the gods' far-flung affairs?
I'll either drive this illicit lust from my heart
or hope to god I die before, and as I lie
languishing in my bed, hope he gives me a kiss . . .
505   But even this needs both parties to want it.
Picture me loving it—while to him, it's a crime.
Aeolus' sons weren't scared to sleep with *their* sisters.
Why do I know this? Why look to such models?
What am I doing? Sick obsession—oh, go;
510   a sister can't love a brother more than is right.
Although . . . if *he'd* been first to fall badly for me,
I might just possibly give in to his love.
So, if I wouldn't say no to him if *he* asked,
I'll ask him. Will I be able to talk? To *tell*?
515   Love makes me: so, yes. Or, if shame seals my lips,
a sealed *letter* can tell him my secret feelings."

She likes this: the thought wins her wavering mind.
She sits up a bit and leans on her elbow.
"Let him see," she whispers. "I'll spill my mad love."
[]521   Shaking, she sets down the words she's considered,

stylus in right hand, wax tablet in left.
She starts but doubts, writes, can't stand what she's written,
makes a mark, rubs it out, revises, loathes, tries again,
puts down what she's taken up, takes up what she's put down.   525
What she wants she doesn't know—then what she's set on
makes her ill. Her face: a flux of daring and shame.
She writes *sister*—but no, better undo sister
and incise the smoothed wax with these words instead:
"To your health!—from one who'll have none if you   530
don't wish it back, one who loves you. Shame, oh shame,
withholds her name! But if you wonder what I wish:
to make my case without my name and, only when
my hopes and prayers are safe, be known as Byblis.
You might have seen signs of the pain in my heart—   535
my paleness and thinness and gaze and wet
eyes, unaccountable sighs, and the urgent
hugs and kisses that, had you paid attention,
you'd know could not be those of a sister.
All the same, though love was causing me pain   540
and I was pure fire inside, I've done all I could
to temper myself (and the gods will agree),
I've fought long and hard to escape Cupid's cruel
weapons, I've suffered worse than you'd ever think
a girl could. But I'm overcome now: I'm compelled   545
to confess and beg your help in my nervous hopes.
You alone can rescue or ruin this lover:
choose which you'll do. It's no enemy who begs,
but one extremely close to you who would love
to be still closer, more intimately entwined.   550
Let old men know laws and ponder what's proper
and right or wrong as they guard the scales of justice.
Love is spontaneous for people our age!
We don't know what's allowed because everything
should be—we make ourselves in the image of gods.   555
No stern father, dread of gossip, or even fear
restrains us: but as there could be reason to fear,
we can cloak our delights as 'brother and sister.'
We already confide to each other in secret;
we're arm in arm always and kiss often outside.   560

What's missing? Pity this girl who spills her love
and never would do so but passion compels her—
and take care not to be *Cause of Death* on my grave."

The tablet was full of such hopeless words traced
565   into the wax, the last line edged to the margin.
She stamped her outrage at once with her seal-ring
and wet it with tears (as her tongue had gone dry).
Blushing with embarrassment, she called for a slave
and sweetly said, "My *most* trustworthy servant . . .
570   take these—" then a long pause "—to my brother."
As she handed him the tablets, they slipped and fell:
upset by the sign, she still sent them. At the right time
the slave drew near and gave him the hidden note.
Caunus took the tablets, read only a bit,
575   then erupted with rage and hurled them away
and could hardly not throttle the trembling slave.
"Go," he shouted, "while you can, you disgusting pimp
of perversion! If what happened to you didn't drag
my honor down, too, you'd pay for this with death."
580   Gray with fear, the slave fled and blurted her brother's
hard words. When Byblis, rejected, heard she went pale,
glacial cold seeping inside and making her shake.
But when her mind returned so did her hopeless craze,
and her tongue scarcely stirred the air with her words:
585   "I deserve this. What made me give tangible proof
of my torment? Why did I so quickly commit
to wax those words that I should have kept hidden?
I should have tried his feelings first, tested him
by hinting. I should have closely studied the winds,
590   seen how they blew with sails *partly* open, in case
they blew against me—and then headed safely
to sea: now my sails billow in unexplored winds.
I founder on rocks, tumble, am overwhelmed
by ocean, and my sails can't turn about.
595   Wasn't I warned by omens to keep my love
private when the tablets fell just as I bid
they be taken, a sign my hopes would fail, too?
Shouldn't the day or the endeavor itself—no,
shouldn't the *day* have been changed? A god warned me

with absolute signs—I was too maddened to see.   600
I should have just spoken, confessed my tormented
feelings in person, not fixed myself in wax.
He'd have seen tears, seen the face of his lover,
and I could have said more than tablets can hold.
I could have thrown my arms around his tense neck,   605
and if he said no, I could have looked set to die,
collapsed at his feet, and pleaded for my life.
I should have done all of that! Each act alone might
not have swayed him, but all together they could.
Or maybe it's the fault of that servant I sent: 610
maybe he didn't approach with tact or choose
the best time or find an open moment or mood.
All this has cost me. For he's no tiger's child,
his heart isn't adamant or obsidian
or stony as flint; he was nursed by no lioness.   615
He *will* be won. I'll try again and never tire
at what I've begun as long as I still breathe.
If I could undo what I've done, then yes: best not
to have started. Next best: carry on now I have.
Even if I gave up my ambitions today,   620
he could never forget what I've already dared.
And if I gave up, I'd only look fickle
or like I'd tried tricking him in some nasty scheme.
Either way I won't seem the prey of that urgent
god who torches our hearts—only lowly lust.   625
So. I can't undo the unspeakable thing done.
I've written, proposed, was too rash with my love.
If I did nothing more, I'd still not be clean.
So there's lots to hope for, little left to go wrong."

She said all this and (her troubled mind was so split)   630
though she was sorry she'd tried, she tried again, went
too far, poor girl, set herself up for rejection.
When there was no end, her brother abandoned
horror and home to found a new city abroad.
They say pitiful Byblis really lost her mind   635
then: she actually ripped the dress from her breast
and in a wild frenzy she hit her own arms.
Deranged, she told everyone of her illicit

love; she deserted her land and hated home
640   and set off to track the trail of her brother.
Like the Maenads you rouse with a thyrsus, Bacchus,
so that they swarm in your triennial rites,
just like that Byblis howled over fields—the ladies
of Bubasis saw her. From there she wandered
645   to Caria, warlike Leleges, and Lycia,
past Cragus, Limyre, the waters of Xanthus,
where the Chimaera with its lion's head and chest
and snake tail below squats on a ridge, breathing fire.
The woods were thin when Byblis fell to the ground,
650   exhausted by chasing. She lay with hair scattered,
her face pressed into the crumpled dry leaves.
The nymphs of Leleges kept trying to lift her
in their tender arms, to show her how to heal
her aching love and soothe her stricken soul.
655   But Byblis lay still, digging her nails into green
moss, wetting the grass with a trickle of tears.
They say the Naiads gave her a vein of fresh tears
that would never go dry; what more could they give her?
Soon—as drops weep from the trunk of a pine tree
660   or oily bitumen oozes from soil
or ice loosens to liquid under the sun
when a warm breeze gently breathes from the west,
so Byblis slowly resolved into tears, slowly
she slipped into stream. In those valleys it still bears
665   her name and springs from the roots of a black oak.

· IV . 2

MYRRHA (10.298–502)

"The son of Paphos was Cinyras, and if he
had been childless, he might have been happy.
300   I'll sing a dark story: back, daughters and fathers!
Or if my songs enchant your souls, don't trust
me now: do not believe this song is true.

But if you do: trust too the acts were punished.
If nature permits something so misbegotten,
I praise the people of Thrace, our part of the world,   305
I compliment this land that's far from those that bred
something so obscene. Let Panchaia bear balsam
and cinnamon, costum and frankincense bleeding
from trunks and all its flowers, too, if it only
bears its myrrh: that new tree was not worth the price.   310
Cupid denies his arrows injured you, Myrrha,
he insists his love-torches did not cause your crime.
A Fury scorched you, a Fury clutching swollen snakes
and sticks dipped in Styx. A crime to hate your father,
yes: but your love's more criminal than hate.
                                            "The best   315
young men in the world want you, Myrrha; princes
of Asia all jostle to wed you. Among these men
please pick one—only *one* can't be among them.
Myrrha can feel her sick passion and is appalled.
'What am I thinking?' she whispers. 'What do I want?   320
Gods, please—and decency, holy family law—
please stop this unspeakable thing, block this crime.
If it really is a crime . . . Yet virtue won't quite
condemn my desire: for animals mate without
such distinction. No one cares if a bull mounts   325
his heifer, a filly can mate with her sire,
a goat ruts among flocks he fathered, and a bird
can conceive with the same seed that spawned her.
They're so lucky, so free! Civilized humans
have made nasty rules: what nature allows   330
jealous laws forbid. But I've heard of places
where son sleeps with mother, daughter with father,
and family values only double the love.
My awful luck that I wasn't born there,
that I'm in the wrong place. But why dwell on this?   335
Obscene longings—go! Yes, he's worth loving:
but only as father. Of course, if I were not
Cinyras' child I could be Cinyras' lover . . .
Because he's mine, he can't be mine; I lose
by being near him. I'd be stronger as a stranger.   340
It'd be better to go, abandon my homeland—

I'd flee this crime. But strong longing keeps me, in love,
so that I can look at him, touch him, talk to him,
too, and sidle near him for a kiss, if no more . . .
345   Evil girl! You really hope to do something more
and don't see all the laws and names you conflate?
You'd be your mother's rival, your father's lover?
Your own son's sister, and your brother's mother?
You're not scared of Furies with black snakes in their hair,
350   those sisters the guilty see jab flaming torches
at their faces and eyes? No: while your body's still
blameless, don't nourish this filth in your heart,
don't foul natural law with prohibited lust.
Yes, you want him: but the facts block you. He's moral,
355   he follows the rules. But oh how I wish he burnt, too!'

"Now Cinyras, given all the girl's suitors,
wasn't sure what to do. To see what she thought
he went over the names: which would she marry?
First she was silent, gazing intent at her father's
360   face, so hot with longing warm tears filled her eyes.
Cinyras, taking this as a young girl's alarm,
said not to cry and dried her cheeks, kissed her lips.
This made Myrrha so glad . . . and when asked what *kind*
of man she would like, she murmured, 'One like you.'
365   He was pleased with words he did not understand. 'Stay
such a good girl forever,' he said. At the word *good*
she dropped her eyes, this girl well aware of her sin.

"Midnight now, when sleep settles bodies and cares:
but Cinyras' child can't sleep. She's incandescent
370   with impossible want, her wild desires brand new.
First she's desperate, then desperate to try, is ashamed,
full of longing, doesn't know what to do. As when
a great tree is hacked by axes, one stroke to go—
which way will it fall?—on all sides they're anxious—
375   just like this, her mind is so weakened it wavers:
she goes this way, then that, then both ways at once.
No hope or relief for her love except death.
Death sounds right. So she gets up to slip a noose
on her neck, loops her wide sash over a beam.

'Goodbye, dear Cinyras. Know you're why I die,'   380
she whispers, and drapes the cord round her wan neck.

"They say that her murmuring words reached the ears
of the faithful nurse sitting watch at her door.
The old woman leaps up, charges the door, sees
the trappings of suicide—and at once shrieks,   385
strikes her breast, tears her dress, and pulls the rope
loose from her baby's neck. Only then is there time
to cry and clasp her and ask why the noose.
The girl sits silent, says nothing, stares at the floor,
sorry that her try was too late and got caught.   390
The old woman persists, shows her gray hair and slack
breast, and begs by the girl's crib and first taste of milk
that Myrrha confide her troubles. The girl moans
and looks off, but the nurse is set on finding out
and assures not only her confidence. 'Tell me,'   395
she says, 'and let me help: I'm old but not useless.
If it's madness, I'll cure you with chanting and tricks;
if it's a hex, I'll purge you with magical rites;
if a god's angry, anger's soothed by sacrifice.
What else can it be? Your household affairs   400
are sound and safe, your mother and father thrive.'
At the word father Myrrha lets out a slow sigh.
Still the nurse can't quite fathom anything wrong
in her mind, but she senses it's some kind of love.
Determined to know, she insists Myrrha tell her   405
the story and pulls her, weeping, onto her lap.
She wraps her weak old arms around the girl and says
'I know: you're in love. In a matter like this I'll be
useful (no fear)—and your father will know nothing
about it.' The maddened girl leaps from her lap, hides   410
her face in a pillow. 'Please go,' she says. 'Leave my
shame to myself. Please go,' she cries, 'or stop asking
what's wrong. It's a crime, what you're trying to know.'
The old woman shudders, holds out hands trembling
with age and fear, and kneels to plead at her baby's feet.   415
She first soothes the girl and—when she still won't confess—
scares her, says she'll report the noose and near-death,
again promises help if she'll just spill her love.

The girl raises her head, wets the old woman's chest
420   with her tears, keeps trying to tell, but keeps falling
silent, finally hides her flushed face in her dress
and says, 'Oh mother, with such a fine mate!'
Just that, and she moans. A chill tremor seeps
through the limbs and bones of the nurse (who knows now,
425   she knows); her frizzled white hair stands on end, stiff.
She says all she can to drive off this foul love,
and the girl knows she's warned, so rightfully warned,
but swears she'll die if she can't have what she wants.
'Then live,' the nurse says. 'Have your—' she can't say
430   "father," says no more, but vows to keep her word.

"The mothers were holding the rites of pure Ceres,
draping their bodies in chalky white gowns
and offering garlands of wheat as first fruits,
and for nine nights they prohibited love, refused
435   the touch of men. With the women was Cenchreis,
wife of the king, observing the sacred rites.
Once his legal mate had left his bed lonely,
the wily old nurse found Cinyras, drunk.
She spoke of a girl who loved him truly (the name
440   she gave was false), called the girl a beauty. How old?
'The same,' she said, 'as Myrrha.' Sent to fetch her,
she hurried home and cried, 'Be glad, my child:
we've won!' But the troubled girl wasn't glad in all
of her heart; part of her sickened with dread.
445   Yet still she thrilled . . . her mind was so riven.

"The time of night when all is still. Between the Bears
Boötes steers his Wagon aslant from the pole:
Myrrha steps toward her crime. The radiant moon flees
the sky, sooty clouds cover shy constellations,
450   night dims without stars. Icarius first hides his face,
then his daughter Erigone, holy with love.
Three times Myrrha stumbles, a sign, and she pauses;
three times a funeral-owl cries the alarm.
Still she walks on, shadows and dark dissolving her shame.
455   One hand grips her nurse as the other hand probes
her dark path. Now she touches the bedroom step,

now she opens the doors, now she's inside. But now
her knees tremble and give, blood drains from her face,
her consciousness flickers as she steps onward.
The closer to ruin she is, the more shocked—she's   460
sorry she dared this, wants to stop while unknown
and pulls back—but the old woman leads her by hand
to the bed, whispers, 'Take her, Cinyras, she's
yours,' and presses the doomed bodies together.

"Then the father pulls into bed his own child,   465
obscene, and soothes the girl's worries, comforts her fears.
Maybe, she's so young, he calls her *Baby*; maybe
she calls him *Daddy*, too—so names will seal the crime.
Then, full of her father, the girl slips away, evil
seed between her cursed legs: the sin is now made flesh.   470
The next night, again—and this isn't the end.
Then Cinyras, dying to know his bedmate
after all these nights of love, lights a lamp and sees
both his daughter and crime. Mute with horror
he pulls his bright sword from the sheath on the wall.   475
But Myrrha escapes death and flees, thanks to night's
darkness and shadows. She wanders wide fields, leaving
behind the Araby palms and groves of Panchaia.
The horns of the moon have swollen nine times
when she rests at last in Sabaea, exhausted,   480
scarcely bearing her belly's weight. Unsure what to wish,
torn between her dread of death and misery in life,
she utters this prayer: 'Oh, if any spirit will hear
my confession, I deserve punishment and won't
resist. But if alive I offend the living   485
and dead I offend the dead, throw me from both zones:
change me. Deny me both life and death.'
Some spirit was open to her words, some god
willing to grant her last prayer. For soil spread
over her shins as she spoke, and her toenails split   490
into rootlets that sank down to anchor her trunk.
Her bones grew dense, marrow thickened to pith,
her blood paled to sap, arms became branches
and fingers twigs; her skin dried and toughened to bark.
Now the growing wood closed on her swollen womb   495

and her breast and was encasing her throat—
but she couldn't bear to wait anymore and bent
to the creeping wood, buried her face in the bark.
Her feelings have slipped away with her form
500   but still Myrrha weeps, warm drops trickling from the tree.
Yet there's grace in these tears: the myrrh wept by the bark
keeps the girl's name, which will never be left unsaid."

· IV . 3

HIPPOLYTUS (15.497–546)

"If you've ever heard of Hippolytus, who died
a hideous death thanks to his stepmother's lie
and father's gullibility—you'll be stunned: I
500   can't prove it, but that's me. My stepmother (Pasiphaë's
child) tried making me foul my father's bed, but no.
Then—stung by rejection? afraid she'd be caught?—
she reversed the crime, accused *me* of wanting
what *she* really did. My father threw me—guiltless!—
505   out of town and cursed me horribly as I left.
In my car I drove for Pittheus' town Troezen,
was passing the coast of the Corinthian bay,
when suddenly up raged the sea: a massive wave
grew and curled high—it looked like a mountain—
510   and it thundered and rose to a splitting peak.
A horned bull burst from the wave as it crashed
then reared up chest-high in the filmy salt air,
snorting seawater from his nostrils and mouth.
My friends' hearts went faint, but I wasn't scared, too
515   distracted by exile. Then my high-strung horses
turned toward sea and grew tense, ears stiff, terrified
by the horrific sight. They panicked and charged
toward the cliff with the car. In desperation
I struggled to hold the reins slickened with foam
520   and strained at the halters, lying all the way back.
And the horses' frenzy would not have outdone me

if a wheel that ought to turn smooth on its axle
hadn't snapped on a stump and gone spinning.
I'm both thrown from the car and tangled in reins—
you'd see organs ripped out, sinews stuck to a post,   525
one arm wrenched loose but the other bound back,
bones splitting and cracking until at last my poor
finished soul sighs out, and you wouldn't know one
bit of this body: it was all a raw, red wound.
Now, could you, nymph—dare you!—possibly compare   530
my disaster to yours? I saw the lightless world
below and washed my torn self in the Phlegethon,
and without Apollo's son's fabulous potions
I would be there still. But once I'd recovered
with treatments and herbs (though Dis didn't like it)   535
Diana wrapped me in fog, so the sight of me
and my gift of new life wouldn't rouse resentment.
So I'd be safe and would look unhurt, too,
she made me older, changed my face so no one
would know me. She thought awhile whether Delos   540
or Crete would be my home, but abandoned both
and set me down here. She made me surrender
my old name as well, my name that spoke of horses.
'Once Hippolytus,' she said, 'you're now Virbius.'
Since then I've lived in this grove as a minor god,   545
devoting myself to my mistress, Diana."

V. *Switching*

TIRESIAS (3.316–338)

As these (fated) events took place down on earth
and double-born Bacchus slept safe in his crib,
it seems that Jove, a little loosened by nectar,
shook off his tribulations to tease and joke
320 with Juno. "I'm convinced," he said, "that women feel
far more than men—I mean, in the joys of sex."
She said no. So they agreed to find out what
Tiresias thought, as he'd known both sides of love.
In greening woods one day he'd seen a pair of snakes
325 entwined and struck them with his walking stick—
then changed from man to woman (true!) and spent
seven falls that way. On the eighth she saw the snakes
again and said, "If striking you has mystic strength
to change the sex of whoever has struck,
330 well then, I'll hit again." She struck the snakes:
former form returned, his own born shape came back.
Now, asked to judge the teasing spat he confirmed
that Jove was right. They say this angered Juno
far more profoundly than seemed right or just:
335 and in the judge's eyes she cast permanent night.
But Almighty Jove (though no god can *undo*
what another god's done) paid for sight stolen
with skill to foresee, an honor to lessen the loss.

IPHIS AND IANTHE (9.666–797)

Talk of the newest dark marvel would have flown
through every town on Crete, if Crete hadn't borne
its own fresh wonder: the case of Iphis transformed.
In Phaestus, near the royal town of Cnossos,
there once lived an unknown fellow named Ligdus,   670
a man of humble stock. His worth was no more grand
than his bloodline, but he led a life blameless
and true. When his wife was pregnant and about
to give birth, he came and gave her this warning:
"Two things I pray: giving birth won't hurt you much   675
and you have a boy. The other sort's harder;
luck gives her little strength. Although I hate this,
if it turns out that you deliver a girl
(god forgive me for saying it)—she must die."
As he said this, tears ran down both their cheeks,   680
his as he ordered her and hers as she heard.
Still, Telethusa begged her husband with useless
pleading not to make her trim her hopes by half,
but Ligdus' decision was final. Now she could
scarcely bear her pregnant belly's mighty weight   685
when at midnight, while she was deep in a dream,
the goddess Isis with a host of holies stood
by her bed, or *seemed* to. At her brow were crescent
horns, a crown of golden wheat, and a queenly
diadem; by her side stood god-dog Anubis,   690
holy Bubastis, Apis with his mottled hide,
and the god who bids silence by touching his lips;
there were rattles, Osiris ever sought by Isis,
and a strange snake plump with poison for sleep.
But *she'd* surely shaken sleep and saw with clear eyes   695
when Isis said, "Telethusa, you're one of mine,
don't worry so; just ignore your husband's demand.
Don't hesitate once Lucina's set the child free:

raise it, whatever it is. I'm a goddess who helps
700   those who ask me: you haven't worshipped my spirit
in vain." So she spoke and dissolved from the room.
Telethusa rose from bed happy, held blameless
hands to the stars, and prayed that her vision come true.

When the pains sharpened and her burden pushed out
705   and to an unwitting father a girl-child was born—
her mother blithely bid the baby *boy* be fed.
The trickery held: just the nurse knew the secret.
The father kept a vow by naming the baby
for Grandfather Iphis. The name pleased the mother:
710   it went both ways; she'd betray no one by using it.
Therefore lies lay hidden in virtuous deceit.
The child dressed as a boy, and whether you saw boy
or girl in the face—each way, it was exquisite.

Thirteen years passed, Iphis, and your father promised
715   you Ianthe, a golden girl wildly praised
among the Phaestian woman for the lushness
of her beauty, the child of Telestes of Crete.
The two had the same age and same looks; the same
teachers had taught them their letters and numbers.
720   Love struck each fresh heart and gave each the same
longing—but in hopes they were far from the same.
Ianthe wants her wedding, bridal torches and all,
certain the one she takes for a man will *be* one.
Iphis loves, too, but can't hope to savor that love,
725   and this kindles her hotter, girl burning for girl.
Barely holding back tears, she says, "What will become
of me, smitten with this freakish, unheard of new
[]728/9   love? If the gods had wanted to ruin me, they
730   could just have given me a natural problem.
Cows don't itch for cows, or mares for other mares.
A ram craves a ewe; a hind follows her stag.
Birds mate like this, too—in the animal world
no female's overcome with lust for a female.
735   I wish I just *weren't*! In case there's some monster Crete
didn't yet have, Pasiphaë fixed her heart on a bull.
But that was female-on-male, and my love's truly

more brainsick than that. Even *she* could quench her
desire; even she—with tricks and a concocted cow—
got her bull, and the cheater's the one who was taken.   740
If all the world's cleverness poured down upon me
or Daedalus flew his wax wings right here, what
could he do? Make a boy of this girl with clever
contraptions? Or is it *you* he'd change, Ianthe?
Pull yourself together, Iphis. Toughen your soul.   745
Give up this stupid obsession, this hopeless hope.
You see what you are. Or do you fool yourself, too?
Want what you ought to—love what a girl should.
It's hope that breeds love and hope that feeds love
but circumstances stop it. No guardian bars   750
you from her sweet arms, no fear of jealous husband
or forbidding father: even she won't say no.
Still you can't have her or be glad, even if it all
went your way and men and the *pantheon* helped you!
What I want, my father wants, and she and hers, too.   [[]]757
Only nature's opposed: omnipotent nature
is all that destroys me. Look—it's nearly time,
the wedding day, when Ianthe should be mine—   760
but won't. So much water and no drop to drink.
Why would Juno or Hymen come to a wedding
with no groom in charge and us both wearing veils?"

At this she falls silent. The other girl tosses, too,
yet she prays that Hymen come as fast as he can.   765
Telethusa's anxious, keeps delaying the day:
she puts it off with made-up illness, cites omens
or visions as excuse. But at last she's used up
her whole stock of stories, and the postponed date
is pressing close: only one day left. She pulls   770
the headband from Iphis' hair and her own,
then with locks flung wild she clutches the altar
and cries, "Isis, you of Paraetonium, the fields
of Mareotis, Pharos, and the antlering Nile,
I beg you, please help us and undo our fears.   775
You, goddess—I saw you once, saw your cymbals
and signs, and I took to heart your advice.   []778
That this girl is alive and I'm not punished—oh,

780   this was your bidding and gift. Pity us both, please,
and help us." Tears flowed right after her words.
The goddess seemed to nudge her altar (it jiggled!),
the temple doors rattled, her moonlike horns glowed,
and the cymbals jangled—yes, you could hear them.

785   Not sure yet but happy with these promising signs
Telethusa leaves the temple. Iphis goes, too,
but with a longer stride than usual, with cheeks

less pale and limbs more strong and a face that seems
tougher and hair that's grown tousled and short,

790   plus more forcefulness than a girl's likely to have.
The girl you were is a boy! Heap gifts in the temple,
don't be shy, rejoice! They do heap gifts in the temple
and add a plaque, and the plaque has a little verse:
A • BOY • FULFILLS • WHAT • A • GIRL • PROMISED • • IPHIS.

795   The next morning, sunrays lit open the world
as Venus, Juno, and Hymen convened
at the wedding, and Iphis got his Ianthe.

• V . 3

ORPHEUS AND EURYDICE (10.1–85)

Hymen flew in yellow robes through fathomless
sky, he flew from Crete for the shores of Thrace,
summoned there by Orpheus—though it was in vain.
Indeed he came, but he brought no holy vows

5   or glowing looks or happy-ever-after hopes.
The torch he held hissed smoke that stung people's
eyes and even shaken could not hatch a flame.
The omen's outcome was even worse: as the bride
strolled the lawns with her handmaiden nymphs, she

10   suddenly fell down dead (snakebite to the ankle).
Once the Thracian singer had wept her enough
in the airs above, to be sure he tried the shades
as well he crept through the Taenarus gates down to Styx.
Through feathery forms and ghosts of the grieved he sought

Proserpina and the prince of that pleasureless   15
place of shadows. Strumming in time with his words,
he sang: "Oh mystic spirits of the world below,
where everyone mortal eventually goes,
if you'll let me tell truth with no riddles or lies
I've crept down here not so I might spy on murky   20
Tartarus or try to tie the triple throats
of that hound whose fur squirms (shocking) with serpents.
I've come for my wife, who stepped on a poisonous
snake and was bitten, plucked just as she bloomed.
I wanted strength to endure and truly have tried—   25
but Amor's won. In upper zones this god's well known;
if this is true here, I don't know. But I suspect,
if the tale of that ancient kidnap is true, Amor
joined the two of you, too. By this place full of fear
and endless Chaos and this realm's silent wastes,   30
I beg you reweave Eurydice's unraveled fate.
We are all consigned to you. We might delay,
but later or sooner we stream to one place;
we wend this way, it's our final abode—
your domain over us mortals lasts longest.   35
When she's old and has traveled her share of years,
you will have her, too; I want only a loan.
But if fate won't grant my wife's release, I will not
go back myself. Be glad for the deaths of us both."

As he sang these words, keeping time with his chords,   40
all the bloodless souls wept: Tantalus did not strain
toward his sinking pool, Ixion's wheel stood stunned,
vultures lifted beaks from liver, the Danaides'
urns dripped dry, and Sisyphus—you sat on your rock.
They say even the Furies were undone by the song,   45
and virgin tears wetted their cheeks. Neither queen
nor netherworld king could say no to his pleas, so they
called Eurydice. She drifted with the newer
shades, and as she came she dragged her swollen foot.
The Thracian hero received wife on condition: 50
he not turn back to look at her until he'd left
Avernus' depths—or the gift would be in vain.

The path through the wordless quiet was steep, dim,
and difficult, the air thick and choking with fog.
55   They had almost reached the Upperworld's rim
when, loving and anxious that she'd slipped, he needed
to see her so turned his eyes. At once she sank back—
arms flung out straining to catch or be caught—
in anguish he grasped only intangible air.
60   Dying again she blamed her husband for nothing
(blame him for what—having loved her so much?)
and she called a last "farewell" that barely brushed
his ears, then dissolved into what she had been.

Orpheus was numbed by his wife's double death—
65   like the man who saw Cerberus' trio of heads,
the middle neck in chains, and his fear only left
when his nature did, his body chilling to stone;
or like Olenos, who chose to seem the guilty
one so took your blame, Lethaea, when you were too
70   proud of your looks—your two hearts once so warmly
conjoined are now rocks on misty Mount Ida.
Orpheus pleaded and begged to pass back below,
but the ferryman said no. So for seven days
he squatted squalid on the banks and didn't eat
75   but fed on his grief and tears and aching heart.
He called the gods of Erebus cruel, then trudged
the slopes of wind-bitten Rhodope and Haemus.

The sun had rounded the year's zones three times
and hung in watery Pisces, and Orpheus shunned
80   womanly love: because for him it had ended
badly or he'd promised to be true. Yet many
women longed for him, and many, scorned, were hurt.
In fact he was first to show Thracian men how
to transfer their love to slender boys, young boys,
85   and pluck those first flowers, the quick spring of youth.

• V . 4

CAENIS (12.146–209)

The warfare and slaughter gave way to peace
for many days; each side dropped arms to rest.
While one wakeful guard watched the Phrygian walls
and one just as wakeful watched the pits of the Greeks,
time for a holiday: Achilles (who'd just killed   150
Cycnus) made Athena glad by now killing a cow.
Once its innards were strewn on the crackling altar
and the sizzle and smoke the gods love filled the sky,
the divines had their due; the rest—on the table.
The top men lounged on cushions and gorged themselves   155
on roasted meat, quelling thirst and worries with wine.
But that night it wasn't songs they sang or lutes
or long, finger-holed boxwood flutes that beguiled
them, but stories, and manly courage was the tales'
theme. They recounted tactics, theirs and their foes',   160
and loved living again the dangers they'd faced and
overcome. What else would Achilles talk about—
what else could they talk about, with great Achilles there?
The latest conquest came up most: how Cycnus
had been beaten. It struck them as astonishing   165
that his young flesh could not be pierced by a spear
or even cut: in fact, it dulled the sword-blades.

Achilles was pondering this, all the Greeks were,
when Nestor said, "In your day there's just one man
who shrugs at blades and no stabbing can slash: 170
Cycnus. But I've seen a man endure a thousand
cuts with no harm to his flesh, Thessaly's Caeneus,
Caeneus of Thessaly, a fabled figure
of Mount Othrys. And his most fabulous feature?
He'd been born a girl." Every man there was thrilled   175
by this horror and urged him tell, Achilles as well:
"Go on and tell us," he said, "fine-talking fellow,

wise man of our age. We're all craving to hear
who Caeneus was, why the big alteration,
180   and which battles you knew him in, fighting whom,
and who he was beaten by, if he was beaten."
The old man said, "Groggy age might dull me now
and much I saw years ago has drifted away,
but there's a good deal I recall. Of all events
185   at war and home nothing's stayed more in my mind,
and if a sprawling long life means that a man
can see a world of things, I've already lived
two hundred years and now am living a third.

"Elatus' child Caenis was famously pretty,
190   Thessaly's most gorgeous girl. In every town—
yours, too, Achilles (it was her town as well)—
she was hopelessly wanted by hopeful men.
Maybe Peleus would have tried to marry her, too,
but he'd just married your mother or at least
195   was engaged. Anyway, Caenis wouldn't wed
at all, but, taking a walk on an empty beach,
she was taken by force by the sea-god (they say).
Once Neptune had fully enjoyed his fresh lust
he told her, 'Anything you'd like, you'll have it.
200   Pick whatever you want!' (Or so goes the tale.)
'This outrage,' said Caenis, 'makes me wish really hard
not to bear it again. Change me from a girl:
you'll grant what I want.' The last words were uttered
in such a deep tone, the voice seemed like a man's—
205   and it was. For the god of the sea had granted
the wish and done more: Caeneus could not be hurt
by a stabbing and would never fall to a sword.
Caeneus left, glad with his gift, and spent his life
in manly pursuits, roaming the fields of Thessaly."

Notes to the Selections from Amores

I.3

The divine figures in this poem are identified indirectly: Venus as Cytherea (4); Apollo as Phoebus, the Muses as Apollo's nine companions, Bacchus as the inventor of the vine (11); and the Fates as sisters who spin out a person's thread of life (17).

21–24: Ovid's accounts of Io (who is accosted and then turned into a heifer by Jove) and of Europa (seduced by Jove in the form of a bull) are included in the following selections from *Metamorphoses* (II•1 and II•3); the girl fooled by a swan (again, Jove in disguise) was Leda.

26: Note how the subject of what will last "forever" has transformed from the start of this poem to its end.

I.4

7: When Hippodameïa married Pirithous, king of the Lapiths, the neighboring Centaurs were invited to the wedding; drunk, they tried to carry off her and other women, leading to a fight. Ovid refers to the same incident in *Am.* 2.12.

59: A standard expression of grief is *me miserum!*—"unhappy me!" Closer in tone and frequency to contemporary English is "Oh, god!"

I.5

1: This poem portraying a (possibly fantastical?) sexual encounter opens with a piece of scene setting typical of subsequent sexual stories in *Metamorphoses*: *aestus erat*, or "It was hot . . ." Here the dreamy male speaker seeks rest from the heat and is discovered by Corinna; in later stories beginning with heat, Callisto is spotted by Jove (these selections, II•2); Arethusa is detected by river-god Alpheus (I•6); Actaeon wanders fatally into Diana's grove (I•3) . . .

11-12: Semiramis was a legendary queen of Assyria, famous for her fabulous political and sexual powers. Lais was a renowned Greek courtesan.

2.12

9-10, 17–18: Paris, prince of Troy, seduced Helen away from her husband, Menelaus. This launched the Trojan War, in which Menelaus and his brother, Agamemnon (the two of them being the Atrides, or sons of Atreus), fought Troy for ten years. "The chief" here refers to one of the Atrides. On lines 17 and 18, Ovid inflates Greece and Troy to be "Europe" and "Asia."

19–20: See note to *Am.* 1.4, line 7.

21–22: Latinus was a king of the Latins (in Italy) and the father of Lavinia, whom he'd originally promised to a local prince, Turnus. But, following a prophecy, Latinus married Lavinia instead to newly arrived Aeneas, provoking war.

23–24: To provide the early (male) settlers of Rome with wives, founder Romulus orchestrated the abduction of neighboring Sabine women.

3.4

19–20: The story of Io, guarded by hundred-eyed Argus, is among the *Metamorphoses* selections in this volume (II•1), although here Ovid offers a different version of the story by introducing Amor.

21–22: Danaë was locked up by her father, King Acrisius, so she could never become pregnant because her child was prophesied to kill the king. But Jove got in by turning himself into a shower of gold, and Danaë later gave birth to Perseus. (For more on him, see I•5.)

23–24: Penelope, Odysseus' wife, fended off suitors and stayed true to Odysseus for the twenty years that he was at war in Troy and lost as he sailed home.

37–40: Ilia was a Vestal Virgin who became mother, by Mars, of Rome's founders Romulus and Remus.

3.11

6: The narrator says that "late horns have appeared on his brow," meaning that he has only lately acquired a bullish strength. Because in English "having horns" means being a cuckold, I've shifted the image south, to the spine.

(b) 37: The brackets indicate that I have followed textual editor E. J. Kenney's decision that lines 35 and 36, appearing in various Latin manuscripts of this text, do not belong in the best possible version of the manuscript, so I have left them out of this translation. *Am.* 3.11 is sometimes presented as a single piece and sometimes as a twin set: hence the double numbering system of the lines.

3.12

13. For "poems" Ovid uses *carmina*, the same word he used in *Am.* 1.3, line 19, which can also mean songs, chants, spells, incantations. These are used, for instance, to create transformations in the story of Glaucus and Scylla (III•6 in these selections, *Met.* 13.952 and 14.58), and likewise, the *carmina* of Ovid's lover have wrought a change over these three books of *Amores*.

21–40: A mini-catalogue of mythical fabrications; many stories mentioned here elliptically are later developed in *Metamorphoses*.

21–22: In *Metamorphoses*, Ovid distinguishes between the two Scyllas that he here combines: one Scylla betrays her father, Nisus, by cutting his magic hair (III•3); the other is hideously transformed by Circe (III•6).

23–24: Perseus has wings on his sandals, as does Hermes; Medusa has snaky hair; Perseus rides the winged horse, Pegasus, which was born of Medusa's blood when Perseus cut off her head. All appear (with different degrees of detail) in "Perseus and Andromeda (and Medusa)," I•5.

25: Tityos tried to rape Latona (Leto), the mother of Apollo and Diana. As punishment, he was stretched and pinned to the ground while two vultures plucked at his liver.

26: The dog is Cerberus, many-headed hound of the Underworld.

27: Enceladon is a giant, more typically given a hundred arms.

28: The "mergirls" are the Sirens with fatally seductive voices, often portrayed as having the faces of women but the bodies of birds; a story about them is included in the longer tale of Proserpina (II•5, that story at *Met.* 5.551–563).

29: The god of winds, Aeolus, confined the opposing ones in a bag to help Odysseus (Ulysses) sail home.

30: Tantalus committed various crimes against the gods (stole their nectar; told their secrets; and served them the flesh of his own son, Pelops, to test them) and was punished by being placed in a pool so that he could reach neither the water he stood in nor the fruit hanging above him and thus was perpetually "tantalized."

31: Niobe boasted that she had more children than Latona and was promptly punished when Latona had her own children (Apollo and Diana) kill all of Niobe's. The bereft mother became a perpetually weeping stone. For Callisto, see II•2.

32: Philomela's story appears in this volume (III•2). Ovid does not here describe her as transformed to a swallow—in some versions of the story, she does become a swallow, and her sister Procne, a nightingale, or the reverse—but given what happens to Itys, I could not resist using the word "swallow" in this context.

33–34: Jove became gold for Danaë, a swan for Leda and an eagle for Ganymede (II•6), and a bull for Europa (II•3).

35: Proteus was a shape-shifting sea-god; the Theban teeth refer to the dragon's teeth sown by Cadmus, which sprang from the ground as armed soldiers.

36: Jason, on his quest for the Golden Fleece, in Colchis was given the task of yoking fire-snorting bulls.

37: After Phaethon, the son of Helios (the Sun), was killed when losing control of his father's fiery chariot, his sisters—now poplar trees—wept tears of amber. Ovid refers obliquely to this incident in "Pygmalion" (I•7).

38: In Vergil's *Aeneid,* the Trojan ships escaped being burned by Turnus (see *Amores* 2.12, lines 21–22) when the goddess Cybele transformed the ships—made of pine trees sacred to her—into sea-nymphs.

39: "The sun that set fast" refers to the sun recoiling in horror at the sight of Atreus serving his brother, Thyestes, the roasted flesh of Thyestes' own children. The incident is part of a complex sequence of crimes and curses beginning with Tantalus (see note to line 30), the grandfather of Atreus and Thyestes, and extending onward through their sons and their own children.

40: Amphion, son of Antiope and Zeus, was a magically powerful lute player whose music alone moved the stones he used to build the walls of Thebes.

Notes to the Selections from Metamorphoses

I.

I . I

ARACHNE (6.1–145)

1: The story that Minerva just heard was told in Book 5, a lengthy tale about a singing contest between the nine daughters of Pierus and the Muses. The Muses naturally won and, to punish the outrageous challenge made by the nine sisters, turned them into magpies. The central story sung by the Muses in this contest is that of Proserpina, with the attendant tale of Arethusa, both included in these selections (II•5 and I•6).

2: Maeonia (also called Lydia) was in the western part of Asia Minor.

9: "Sea-snail purple" was highly prized Tyrian dye extracted from the animal of the murex shell. This is a "Golden Line"—two adjectives, verb, two nouns—all but untranslatable: *Phocaico bibulas tingebat murice lanas.*

15–16: Tmolus is a mountain near the Aegean coast of present Turkey; the Pactolus river flows from it.

70ff: Minerva and Neptune compete over which of the two will name the city later known as Athens; Minerva's Greek name, Athena, makes clear who won.

87–128: Many of the flash myths in both Minerva's and Arachne's weavings tell all of each tale that needs telling here, or almost all we know, this passage being the sole remaining source. Note that Proserpina (114) is not only Jove's victim but also his daughter. The "flaxen mother of wheat" (118) is Ceres; the "snake-haired mother" is Medusa (119).

139: Hecate was an Underworld goddess associated with witchcraft, magic, ghosts, and night.

I . 2

DAPHNE (I.452–567)

453: The Peneus River runs through Thessaly.

454: Python: a monstrous snake that lived near Delphi, on a spur of Mount Parnassus, and which Apollo has just killed. Delphi becomes Apollo's precinct.

480: Hymen: a god of marriage ceremonies.

516: Tenedos, Claros, and Patara are in Asia Minor.

528: A Golden Line freezes Daphne's beauty pictorially: *obuiaque aduersas uibrabant flamina uestes.*

559ff: Daphne has become a laurel tree (or shrub); laurel leaves were used to make crowns for triumphant generals in Rome, and laurel seems also to have been planted by Augustus' doorway.

567: Daphne's story (with its interestingly ambiguous ending) leads directly to that of Io (II•1).

I . 3

ACTAEON (3.138–252)

138: Cadmus (Europa's brother; see II•3) has founded Thebes; married Harmonia (daughter of Venus and Mars); and produced a large, lively family (including a daughter, Semele, III•1).

155: This is southeast of Thebes, near Plataea.

168–71: The six nymphs' names are Greek, and they are lovely Greek names, so most translators leave them that way. But soon to come in the story is a long list of the names of dogs (the "Catalogue of Dogs"), which are also Greek yet usually translated into English, because the meanings are telling and funny. I have likewise translated the Greek names in this mini-catalogue of nymphs, which gives the scene a Disney-like effect that seems to suit Ovid's playful and ever-shifting register of tones in a story that will end up horrific.

252: Actaeon's story leads directly to that of Semele, his aunt (III•1).

I . 4

ECHO AND NARCISSUS (3.339–510)

339: This story follows that of Tiresias (V•1).

342: Cephisos is a river that flows from the northwestern slope of Mount Parnassus through the Boeotian plain, and here also refers to the god of that river.

385: Here Narcissus is "tricked by the sense of an answering voice" (*alternae deceptus imagine vocis*); soon, on line 416, he will be "entranced by the image he sees" (*visae correptus imagine formae*). See Perseus in a similar—yet crucially different—situation (I•5, *Met.* 4.676).

406: Nemesis: a goddess or personification of punishment.

419: Marble from Paros (an island in the Aegean) was fine, pure white, and highly sought for sculpture.

481: A Golden Line again makes pictorial a moment of action: *nudaque marmoreis percussit pectora palmis.*

I.5

PERSEUS AND ANDROMEDA (AND MEDUSA) (4.614–803)

614: The brothers are Perseus and the god Bacchus, both sons of Jove. Jove came to Danäe as a shower of gold and impregnated her with baby Perseus, and he came to Semele (Cadmus' daughter) as his most fiery self and begot Bacchus: see Semele's story, III•1.

615: The horror of snakes is Medusa's severed head; Perseus will tell her story shortly.

617: "Libya" refers more generally to North Africa; "Ethiopia" (on line 669) to the region just below Egypt.

618: The Gorgons were three daughters of Phorcos, usually portrayed as monstrous, and the one singled out here is Medusa. To look at her face is to turn into stone.

625: The Bears are the constellations of Ursa Major and Minor; the Crab, Cancer.

643: Themis: an oracular goddess.

663: See the note to *Amores* 3.12, line 29.

670: Andromeda's mother, Cassiopeia, foolishly compared her own beauty to that of the sea-nymphs, bringing on punishment from the sea.

676: Ovid uses the same Latin phrase when Narcissus sees his reflection (I•4, *Met.* 3.416)— *visae correptus imagine formae.*

717: Another pictorial Golden Line: *squamigeris auidos figit ceruicibus ungues.* The first word here literally means "scale-bearing"; to suggest the aestheticization of the moment, I've used "sequined."

774: These daughters of Phorcos are called the Graiae, or Gray Ones.

I.6

ARETHUSA (5.577–641)

Arethusa's story follows that of Proserpina (II•5). Arethusa tells her own story to Ceres, once Ceres has recovered her daughter (part time) and is in a mood to listen. Yet Arethusa speaks in a tale that is told by Calliope, itself told by an unnamed Muse, in turn told by Ovid's narrating persona recounting the contest between the Muses and the Pierides. This is the most nested of all Ovid's nesting stories.

578: "Achaea" here seems to indicate all the Peloponnese.

585: Stymphalos is in northwest Arcadia, in the Peloponnese.

586: *Aestus erat,* or "it was hot": see note to poem 1.5 of *Amores.*

599: Alpheus is the god of the river likewise named, which runs through Arcadia.

607–8: Orchomenos, etc.: places far-flung across Arcadia. Arethusa runs very far.

640: Ortygia is in Syracuse: Arethusa has swum through channels under the Ionian Sea, an episode she briefly describes within the longer story of Proserpina.

I . 7

PYGMALION (10.243–297)

Orpheus is singing this story; see his own tale (V•3). His professed theme in his long song is "boys / great gods have loved, and girls stunned by illicit / lust who deserved what they got for their passion" (*Met.* 10.152–154). Among those stories: that of Ganymede (II•6), Hyacinth (III•4), Adonis (III•5), and Myrrha (III•8).

243: The women who sicken Pygmalion are the Propoetides, who denied Venus' divinity. As punishment, they were turned first into prostitutes and then into stone. This story is set in Cyprus, Venus' birthplace.

263: For the daughters of Helios (the Sun), see note to *Amores* 3.12, line 37.

284: The honey and wax from Mount Hymettus, near Athens, were prized.

290: The child Pygmalion's dream girl soon bears will be named Paphos, as will the place the child is born—but Pygmalion can only ironically be called a hero, and only anachronistically a *Paphian* hero, at that.

297: This story leads directly to that of Myrrha (III•8).

II.

II . I

IO (1.568–746)

This story follows that of Daphne (I•2).

568–70: The Peneus River is in northwest Thessaly, flowing from Mount Pindus, sometimes called the spine of Greece. The river-god Peneus is Daphne's father.

579: The first four rivers (or streams) flow through Thessaly; the last, through Epirus.

583: The Inachus River flows through the eastern Peloponnese, in the Argolid, and is near the pastures and wooded ranges through which Io runs (line 598).

650: On another case of a physical piece of evidence of an inner state, another printed *indicium*, see Byblis (IV•7, *Met.* 9.585).

669: This son of Jove is Mercury; his mother is Maia, one of the seven sisters called the Pleiades.

689: Arcadia is a remote highland region in the center of the Peloponnese. The home of Pan, god of woods, groves, and wilderness, Arcadia became known as a place of idyllic wilds.

695–96: The "Ortygian goddess" and "Latona's daughter" are ways of naming Diana, who was born in Ortygia to Latona (Leto).

700ff: Note the extraordinarily untold-yet-told story!

722: Juno's bird is the peacock.

II . 2

CALLISTO (2.401–507)

This story follows that of Phaethon, who tried to drive the car of his father, the Sun, but lost control, setting the earth ablaze.

405: On Arcadia, see note to line 689 of Io's story.

415: Maenalus is a mountain range in Arcadia.

459: An aestheticizing Golden Line: *nuda superfusis tingamus corpora lymphis*.

495: Callisto's father is Lycaeon, who was transformed into a wolf for his savagery. Note that this is the second time in Callisto's story that someone might be hiding inside another's body.

499: Erymanthus is a mountain range to the northwest of Arcadia.

II . 3

EUROPA (2.833–875)

833: Aglauros committed two crimes. The first involved Minerva (Pallas) and a baby, Ericthonius. This baby was the magically born son of Vulcan, who had tried to mate with Minerva, but she repelled him and wiped his (sudden) ejaculation onto the earth, which then miraculously performed the female part of procreation. Minerva had the resulting sacred child kept safe in a chest, and Aglauros and her sisters were to care for him but never look at him. In looking at the baby, Aglauros committed a grave crime. Second, Aglauros tried to profit from a sexual affair between her sister, Herse, and the god Mercury. This and her earlier crime so angered Minerva that she had the girl infested by the spirit of Envy so that, through jealousy and spite, Aglauros would do all she could to keep Mercury and his love away from her sister. This in turn angered Mercury so much that he transformed Aglauros to stone.

835: Mercury is leaving the region of Athens.

836: Mercury's father is Jove.

839: The star of Mercury's mother (Maia) is in the constellation of the Pleiades.

840, 845: Sidon and Tyre were part of Phoenicia; Tyre was also the source of the famous purple dye made from murex.

II . 4

HERMAPHRODITUS AND SALMACIS (4.285–388)

This story is told by Alcithoe, one of the three daughters of Minyas, who have refused to take part in the festival of Bacchus that all other women in the region (Boeotia) are celebrating; instead these sisters stay home and weave. To enliven their time working, they tell stories. Alcithoe is the last of the three to tell a tale.

382: Ovid has carefully withheld the character's name until now, instead calling him only the child of Mercury and Venus—that is, the child of Hermes and Aphrodite: hence, Hermaphroditus.

II . 5

PROSERPINA (5.346–576)

An unnamed Muse is telling Minerva the story that another Muse, Calliope, had sung in the contest between Muses and Pierides (see opening note to the story of Arethusa, I•6).

347: Typhon (also Typhoeus) was a monstrous Giant who threatened the gods.

356: The lord of the silent is Dis (also Hades or Pluto), god of the Underworld.

368: The three chief male gods had drawn lots to decide who would rule each part of the world: Jove won the Upperworld, Neptune the sea, and Dis the Underworld, which is also called by its regions, such as Tartarus.

385: Enna is in the center of Sicily; the Cayster, a famous river in Asia Minor.

405ff: Dis is driving them southeast, toward Syracuse.

461: The boy has become a newt.

541: Acheron refers to one of the Underworld rivers, as well as that river's presiding deity.

543: Erebus is primal Darkness, a way of naming the Underworld.

544: Phlegethon is one of the Underworld rivers.

552: Achelous is a river in western Greece; its deity is the father of girls who will become the Sirens.

576: This story glides directly to that of Arethusa (I•6).

II . 6

GANYMEDE (10.143–161)

Orpheus sings this story; see his own (V•3) and the earlier note introducing Pygmalion (I•7). After returning alone from the Underworld, Orpheus (who now prefers boys to women) sits to play his lyre; the music is so exquisite that even shade, trees, and wild creatures come to listen. Just before Ganymede's story, Ovid has presented a brief catalogue of the trees that have circled Orpheus and the history of one, the cypress.

148: Orpheus' mother is the Muse Calliope, who has herself sung stories elsewhere in these selections: see Proserpina and Arethusa (II•5 and I•6).

150–51: Orpheus refers to the battle between the Giants and the gods, battles said to have taken place in the Phlegraean fields, volcanic grounds near Vesuvius.

156: Phrygia is modern Turkey, site of ancient Troy.

161: This story moves directly to that of another boy loved by a god, Hyacinth (III•4).

III.

III . I

SEMELE (3.253–315)

This story follows that of Actaeon, who was Semele's nephew; see that story (I•3), as well as Europa's (II•3).

258: Jove's Tyrian pet (*paelex*, concubine or mistress) is Europa.

272: The Styx is the chief Underworld river.

314: Nysa is possibly in India but certainly east, and this twice-born baby raised abroad is Bacchus.

315: This story leads directly to that of Tiresias (V•1).

III . 2

TEREUS, PROCNE, AND PHILOMELA (6.424–673)

424: Athens had been besieged by unspecified seafaring warriors, and Tereus had come to the aid of the Athenian king, Pandion. Tereus was from Thrace, to the northeast.

430: The Furies, also called Erinyes or Eumenides, are primal beings that avenge crimes, especially those against family ties or involving broken oaths.

670: Although I have had to use different words in English, Ovid uses the same word, *notas*, for the figures, letters, or images that Philomela weaves into her cloth (line 577), and for the markings on the new-made birds.

III . 3

SCYLLA (8.6–151)

6: Minos was king of Crete, and the son of Jove and Europa (II•3), as well as the stepfather of the monstrous Minotaur, which his wife, Pasiphaë, conceived with a bull. Megara: a port city on the south coast of Attica.

29: Ovid uses the same phrase—*iunctam cum viribus artem*—to describe Apollo in the story of Hyacinth (III•4, *Met.* 10.181).

100: Crete in fact already has a famous monster—Minos' stepson—and Iphis' story also treats the idea of monsters on Crete (V•2).

121: Charybdis is an infamous whirlpool near the Straits of Messina; Odysseus (and other travelers) had to sail between it and Scylla (not the antiheroine of this story but the one transformed by Circe into a sea monster, with dogs growing from her hips: III•6).

III . 4

HYACINTH (10.162–219)

This story follows that of Ganymede (II•6); Orpheus is singing. See the note above introducing Pygmalion (I•7).

165: Aries and Pisces are zodiacal constellations whose relative places in the sky here indicate the end of winter and start of spring.

167: Delphi (sometimes called the navel of the world) was the precinct of Apollo.

210: "Stained" here is *signaverat*, one of many words in this story with connotations of writing: *inscribenda* (199), *auctor* (199, 214), *inscribit* (215), *inscriptum*, *littera* (216).

III . 5

ADONIS (AND ATALANTA) (10.503–739)

This story follows that of Myrrha (IV•2); the child within the tree trunk is the one she conceived with her father. Orpheus is singing; see the note introducing Pygmalion (I•7).

507: Lucina is a goddess of childbirth who helps pregnant women deliver and also a name for Juno when performing this function.

530–31: Favorite places of Venus are the islands of Cythera and Cyprus (Paphos and Amathus) and the Carian seaside town of Cnidos.

686: Echion was one of the men "sown" by Cadmus when he planted dragons' teeth.

712: Ovid (or Orpheus) reminds us that Adonis is both son and grandson of Cinyras, Myrrha's father.

739: The Greek root of *anemone* is *anemos*, or "wind."

III . 6

GLAUCUS AND SCYLLA (13.898–14.69)

Scylla (not to be confused with the other *Metamorphoses* Scylla, Nisus' daughter, III•3) has been talking with Galatea and other sea-nymphs. Galatea has just told her story, in which the boy she loved, Acis, was attacked by jealous Cyclops but miraculously transformed to a river-god.

13.906: Euboea is a region of Greece, a long island running along the east coast.

918: Proteus is a shape-shifting old man of the sea; Triton is a fishtailed merman; Palaemon (son of Athamas and Ino, Semele's sister, III•1) is a young sea god often depicted riding a dolphin.

950: Oceanus is both the river that rings the earth and a Titan; he and Tethys (also a Titan) parented the water-nymphs and river-gods.

968: The story is split between books 13 and 14 of *Metamorphoses*. Circe is a daughter of Helios (the Sun) and sister of Aeetes of Colchis, whose daughter Medea helps Jason take the Golden Fleece and who is, like Circe, an enchantress. In the *Odyssey*, Circe lives on an island and is famous for turning men into animals; with Hermes' help, Odysseus escapes this presumed devolution and becomes Circe's lover for a time.

14.2ff: For Typhon's throat, see the opening to Proserpina's story (II•5). Glaucus is swimming from Sicily, from the Straits of Messina, and west across the Tyrrhenian Sea.

15: Titania is a way of naming Circe, as a daughter of the Sun, who is counted among the Titans.

27: The Sun had been the first to see Venus sleeping (adulterously) with Mars, driving her husband, Vulcan, to devise a trap for the lovers. The story appears in book eight of the *Odyssey*, and Ovid tells it, too, in book four of *Metamorphoses*.

IV.

IV . 1

BYBLIS AND CAUNUS (9.454–665)

Byblis and her brother, Caunus, are twins of astonishing beauty, the children of water-nymph Cyaneë.

498: Ops is a Roman goddess of fertility, sister and wife of Saturn, the two corresponding roughly to the Greek Rhea and Cronus. For Oceanus and Tethys, see the story of Glaucus (III•6), note to 13.950.

507: Book 10 of the *Odyssey* tells of the six sons and six daughters of wind-god Aeolus, children he wed to one another.

585: Byblis has given an *indicium*, a token of physical proof (of her inner state) through writing, just as Io, when still a heifer, gives her father such a token of her inner identity by printing her name in the sand; see II•1, *Met.* 1.650.

645: Byblis wanders southeast in Asia Minor.

665: This story leads to that of Iphis and Ianthe (V•2).

IV . 2

MYRRHA (10.298–502)

Orpheus is singing this story, which follows that of Pygmalion (I•7). Paphos is the baby born to Pygmalion and his sculpture-turned-woman.

305ff: Thrace (the homeland of Tereus, III•2) was considered a land of high passions: a joke for Orpheus to say this. Panchaia is a mythical place rich in spices and far to the east and south.

447: Boötes is a star near the constellation of the Great Bear, or Ursa Major; see the story of Callisto (II•2). That constellation is also called the Wain, or wagon, and Boötes is also called the Wagoner.

450–51: Icarius had been taught by Bacchus to make wine, which he introduced to the local people of Attica. Drunk and feeling they'd been poisoned, they killed Icarius. His daughter Erigone then killed herself out of daughterly devotion. Both were turned into stars.

467–68: In his translation of *Metamorphoses*, Stanley Lombardo translates *filia* and *pater* as *Baby* and *Daddy*. I can't imagine a better rendering so have gratefully adopted his.

502: Myrrha's child will be Adonis; her story leads directly to his (III•5).

IV . 3

HIPPOLYTUS (15.497–546)

Hippolytus is talking to the nymph Egeria, inconsolable after the death of her husband, Numa. Hippolytus is the out-of-marriage son of Theseus and an Amazon, thus the stepson of Theseus' wife, Phaedra. She is the daughter of Minos, king of Crete, and Pasiphaë (the woman who fell in love and mated with a bull—by hiding inside a wooden cow created by the artist Daedalus—and subsequently gave birth to the Minotaur, in turn kept inside a labyrinth Daedalus devised).

506: Troezen is a town in northeast Peloponnese, and Pittheus was Theseus' grandfather.

532: Phlegethon is one of the Underworld rivers. (Proserpina uses its water to turn her tattletale into an owl: II•5, *Met.* 5.544.)

533: Apollo's son, Aesculapius, was raised by the centaur Chiron and learned from him the arts of medicine and healing.

540: Delos is an island within the Cyclades in the Aegean. Where Diana instead settles new-made Hippolytus is in her woods and sanctuary by Lake Nemi, just south of Rome.

V.

V . I

TIRESIAS (3.316–338)

This story follows that of Semele (III•1): Bacchus is the child plucked from Semele's immo-lated body and sewn into Jove's thigh until ready to be born (again).

327: In so many of Ovid's stories of metamorphosis, the inner character remains after the body has been transformed, even if speech is no longer possible: see Actaeon and Io, for instance (I•3 and II•1). Yet occasionally a personal character—a person's thoughts and feelings—also disappears: Myrrha no longer has her sensations, yet the tree she has become weeps (IV•2); the mind of Salmacis, intriguingly, dissolves into the body of the newly biform Hermaphroditus, even though she instigated that change (II•4). Tiresias' own character presumably remains in the new female form, yet should this figure be identi-fied by a female or male pronoun? Ovid can avoid the problem in Latin: harder for us in English. Most translators retain the masculine pronoun even when Tiresias is a woman. I've chosen instead to refer to Tiresias during those seven altered years as "she," because germane to this story is Tiresias' experience of a woman's sensations recollected and expressed in words.

338: This story leads to that of Echo and Narcissus (I•4).

V . 2

IPHIS AND IANTHE (9.666–797)

This story follows that of Byblis (IV•1)

687ff: Isis is an Egyptian goddess associated with female fertility and portrayed with cow imagery (sometimes having the head of a cow); her worship had become popular in Rome by Ovid's time. Her husband and brother is Osiris, who represents male fertility. In an earlier incarnation, Osiris was killed and cut to pieces that were scattered; Isis looked for them and finally gathered and buried them: Osiris became then a figure of death and rebirth as well. Anubis, another Egyptian god, has the head of a dog and escorts souls to the afterlife; Bubastis is a cat-headed goddess; Apis is a bull-god with mystical markings on his hide.

736: For Pasiphaë, see introductory note to Hippolytus (IV•3).

762: Hymen is a god of weddings and marriages.

V . 3

ORPHEUS AND EURYDICE (10.1–85)

This story appears after that of Iphis and Ianthe (V•2).

22: A Golden Line: *terna Medusaei uincirem guttura monstri*. Some depictions of the hell hound Cerberus give him not just three heads but also fur formed of snakes. When Hercules visited the Underworld, he did tie up Cerberus.

41ff: A mini-catalogue of souls in torment in the Underworld. For Tantalus, see *Am.* 3.12, note to line 30. Ixion had murdered a guest, been exonerated by Jove, but then outraged Jove by trying to approach Juno sexually; his punishment was to be bound to an ever-turning (sometimes flaming) wheel. The Giant Tityos had also assaulted a goddess, Latona (Leto), the mother of Apollo and Diana; for this crime he was staked to the ground, a vulture on either side perpetually plucking at his liver. The Danaïdes were sisters married by force, who (at their father's bidding) killed their husbands on their wedding night; for this, they were consigned perpetually to carry water in leaky jars. Sisyphus was a fantastically tricky fellow, king of Corinth, among whose tricks was to cheat Death by chaining him; for his deeds he was punished by having to roll a boulder to the top of a hill, at which point it would roll back down, and so it would go forever.

65ff: What this unnamed man and the figures of Lethaea and Olenos have in common is that all turned to stone.

77: Rhodope and Haemus are mountain ranges in Thrace.

V . 4

CAENIS (12.146–209)

146: The fighting that just ended was one of the Trojan War battles, in which Achilles managed to kill Cycnus—a son of Neptune whose body could not be pierced or cut—by throttling him instead.

193: Peleus is Achilles' father; his mother is the sea-nymph Thetis.

Further Reading

Ancona, Ronnie, and Ellen Green, eds. *Gendered Dynamics in Latin Love Poetry.* Baltimore: Johns Hopkins University Press, 2005.

Boyd, Barbara Weiden, ed. *Brill's Companion to Ovid.* Leiden: Brill, 2002.

Boyd, Barbara Weiden, and Cora Fox, eds. *Approaches to Teaching the Works of Ovid and the Ovidian Tradition.* New York: Modern Language Association, 2010.

Brown, Sarah Annes. *Ovid: Myth and Metamorphosis.* London: Bristol Classical Press, 2005.

Cantarella, Eva. *Bisexuality in the Ancient World.* New Haven: Yale University Press, 2002.

Carson, Anne. *Eros the Bittersweet.* Princeton: Princeton University Press, 1986.

Curran, Leo C. "Rape and Rape Victims in *Metamorphoses.*" *Arethusa* 11 (1978): 213–41.

Enterline, Lynn. *The Rhetoric of the Body from Ovid to Shakespeare.* Cambridge: Cambridge University Press, 2000.

Fantham, Elaine. *Ovid's* Metamorphoses. New York: Oxford University Press, 2004.

———. *Women in the Classical World: Image and Text.* New York: Oxford University Press, 1995.

Hallett, Judith P., and Marilyn B. Skinner. *Roman Sexualities.* Princeton: Princeton University Press, 1997.

Hardie, Philip, ed. *The Cambridge Companion to Ovid.* Cambridge: Cambridge University Press, 2002.

———. *Ovid's Poetics of Illusion.* Cambridge: Cambridge University Press, 2002.

Hinds, Stephen. *The Metamorphosis of Persephone: Ovid and the Self-Conscious Muse.* Cambridge: Cambridge University Press, 1987.

Keith, Alison. *Engendering Rome: Women in Latin Epic.* Cambridge: Cambridge University Press, 2000.

Knox, Peter E., ed. *Oxford Readings in Ovid.* New York: Oxford University Press, 2006.

———. *A Companion to Ovid.* Chichester, UK: Wiley-Blackwell, 2009.

Lefkowitz, Mary. *Women in Greek Myth.* Baltimore: Johns Hopkins University Press, 2007.

Richlin, Amy. "Reading Ovid's Rapes." In *Pornography and Representation in Greece and Rome,* edited by Amy Richlin (Oxford and New York: Oxford University Press, 1992) 158–79.

Rimell, Victoria. *Ovid's Lovers: Desire, Difference and the Poetic Imagination.* New York: Cambridge University Press, 2006.

Salzman-Mitchell, Patricia B. A. *Web of Fantasies: Gaze, Image, and Gender in Ovid's* Metamorphoses. Columbus: Ohio State University Press, 2005.

Segal, Charles. "Ovid's Metamorphic Bodies: Art, Gender, and Violence in the Metamorphoses." *Arion,* 3rd series, 5, no. 3 (Winter 1998): 9–41.

Skinner, Marilyn B. *Sexuality in Greek and Roman Culture.* Oxford: Blackwell, 2005.

Spentzou, Efrossini. *Readers and Writers in Ovid's* Heroides: *Transgressions of Genre and Gender.* New York: Oxford University Press, 2003.

Williams, Craig A. *Roman Homosexuality.* New York: Oxford University Press, 2010.

Acknowledgements

I am enormously grateful to Elaine Fantham and Alison Keith for contributing their expertise and voices to this project, as well as to the team at Oxford University Press who ushered this from proposal to book, above all Charles Cavaliere and Michelle Koufopoulos. Among many scholars, poets, and writers who read parts or the whole along the way and provided encouragement, advice, or gentle correction are Stephen Hinds, David Christenson, Maureen Seaton, John Kirby, Shadi Bartsch, Betty Rose Nagle, Robert Polito, Fred Leebron, Pam Hammons, and all my co-fellows at the University of Miami's Center for the Humanities. I've had extensive support from the University of Miami while preparing these translations, through a Provost Summer Research Award, an Arts and Sciences Career Enhancement Award, and a Center for the Humanities Fellowship, for all of which I am extremely grateful. My thanks also to Karl Kirchwey and the American Academy in Rome for creating a wonderful opportunity to meet other Ovid re-imaginers at "Ovid Transformed: The Poet and the *Metamorphoses*," in May 2013. Finally, my gratitude as ever to Alex, for bearing each translation as it first came to the page.

Credits

Frontispiece: Photograph © 2014 Museum of Fine Arts, Boston
Plate I: Scala / Art Resource, NY
Plate II: Vienna, Kunsthistorisches Museum / The Bridgeman Art Library
Plate III: Image copyright © The Metropolitan Museum of Art. Image source:
    Art Resource, NY
Plate IV: Photograph © 2014 Museum of Fine Arts, Boston
Plate V: © The Trustees of the British Museum / Art Resource, NY
Plate VI: Image copyright © The Metropolitan Museum of Art. Image source:
    Art Resource, NY
Plate VII: Museo Pio Clementino, Vatican / Art Resource, NY
Plate VIII: Louvre, Paris / The Bridgeman Art Library
Plate IX: © Vanni Archive / Art Resource, NY
Plate X: Gianni Dagli Orti / The Art Archive at Art Resource, NY
Plate XI: Scala / Art Resource, NY
Plate XII: Walters Art Gallery, Baltimore
Plate XIII: Photograph © 2014 Museum of Fine Arts, Boston
Plate XIV: Erich Lessing / Art Resource, NY
Plate XV: Erich Lessing / Art Resource, NY
Plate XVI: © Vanni Archive / Art Resource, NY